THE CASE

Also by John Fraser

and published by AESOP Modern:

Animal Tales

Black Masks

Blue Light / Starting Over

Down from the Stars

Enterprising Women

Hard Places

An Illusion of Sun

The Magnificent Wurlitzer

Medusa

Military Roads

The Observatory

The Other Shore

The Red Tank

Runners

Soft Landing

The Storm

Three Beauties

Wayfaring

THE CASE

JOHN FRASER

AESOP Modern Fiction
Oxford

AESOP Modern Fiction
An imprint of AESOP Publications
Martin Noble Editorial / AESOP
28 Abberbury Road, Oxford OX4 4ES, UK
www.aesopbooks.com

First edition published by AESOP Publications

A catalogue record of this book is available from the British Library.

First edition 2013, revised 2014

ISBN: 978-0-9572061-3-7

Printed and bound in Great Britain by
Lightning Source UK Ltd,
Chapter House, Pitfield, Kiln Farm,
Milton Keynes MK11 3LW

The Case

At last my friend Dan thrusts into the bar, as if he's pushed by hot winds. No one seems to follow him. He looks round at other guys making their noise.

'Tongue-slitters!' he says loudly. 'Why do we meet in a torturers' bar?' He sticks out a greyish tongue at them, and slabbers incoherent words: 'Tell them nothing,' he says to me, and laughs: 'They don't know what intelligence can be.'

'They're bankers and such,' I say.

'Well, their liberty's a luxury, waiting for their pensions while their big army does its work,' he says. He turns to me, 'How's your life?'

'It's years since we met – those years have passed and now are silent. I've been spying, on the frontier. The paper that I work for doesn't pay, so there I was in Kičevo, watching the movement.'

He nods, knowing all about Kičevo. He says,

'I saw you talking to that tart, the short one, in the blue aertex combo.'

'She's maybe not quite a tart. Lives round here.'

'That makes no special sense,' says Dan. He chants a little. 'She won't help you break no system down!' Then, 'What we need,' he says confidentially, 'is experts who've read all the books, and run like snakes.

The only way. Not caring who's our followers, or who pays.' He squirms around, to classify the drinking guys, especially their shoes, 'That's how you tell.'

It's like touching a bare wire, with him, and then again, again the spurt of hot, and maybe it will only bring you bad.

'I was with the Indians,' he says, into the blue, then back he turns to me, 'They've understood technology, those phones the guys have given them, and then the movies that they're in. They're far ahead. Of course, they're just a block, no one can pronounce their names. Everything's been lost, for them. They're what we'll be. After the breaking; then we build it up again.'

'You're crazy, Dan,' I say. 'To break it down and build it up? You're into liberalism? Just leave it be.'

'No,' he says, 'I'm really quite indifferent. It's just survival, that is all. There you are, into the jungle, a foul and threatening place, your food is cool and poisonous, and every beetle, every grub, is suffering and all its life will suffer from the screeching of the parrots and its emptying gut, the ghosts behind the trees, the pits that's full of skulls, the suffering of each and all, the moths that eat your eyes, the grass that darts and grows inside your penis – yes, my friend, be sure it's love that sets the whole thing up and makes it spin!'

I say, 'French guys say it's there you feel pure, you contemplate. A friendly margin. No castes, no prize.'

'Well, that just shows crap,' says Dan. 'That's

forest. Jungle – the first time, I was scared, then scared all the time. That's why the Indians don't sing when they're inside. It's not their dinner they are looking for – it's avoiding being someone else's snack. The second time I knew more, I was more scared. And on and on, so. Of course, you love it. It's like a woman – once you've had her, she's had you, and then the only change can be – rejection. There's no compromise. With men, it's different – playacting and doing deals. That's not for me.'

'That's against the run of common sense,' I say.

'Fuck common sense,' he says. 'The thing about your jungle's this – you can reject it, not go back. Or else it can reject you, and you fall into a pit, or hoisted up in nets. Forget the cultural stuff, the woman nurturer – that's all a scam. It – she – gives you what's to eat: you take it, steal it, stab it. Tomorrow – there's the hunger, just the same.'

'It's impressive, Dan,' I say, and that's the truth: 'Why'd you go in? Jungles, Indians, all that?'

'They were teaching me,' he says, perhaps a little cautious now, 'Just venturing how to survive. That's all you need to know. The rest is whitewash,' and I say,

'It all seems stereotype to me. The wisdom, the surviving,' and he says,

'It's life, old friend. You can live through it, all of it, and never know it's life. You've lived, you've died. You think it's something taking you from there to here.

But *here*'s the grave. The road is life. That's the beast you have to wrestle with,' and he leans back upon the bench.

Hohum, I think, and say, 'Well, it does make some sense, but not original or very deep.' Maybe he nods again, he says, 'And then I made some cash, a lot,' and so I say,

'Then lay some out, upon our tab.'

And so he does, a wad rolled tight, a snotty green that smells of skin.

I say, 'Dan, I can't imagine you – sex with men, weighing up accounts,' and he reads me well, says,

'You're right. It's quite delusional, the whole thing, especially the details. That's what puts you off. It's just the women, they are warriors, and they fight wars. The men are only good for skirmishes, and often tears. That warring stuff is for the young guys, really young. For some, a crossroads. But you must plough ahead. Not Indians only – it's true for everyone What I mean – it has to start and end small, otherwise it couldn't be great, magnificent. So, when you are a big shot, you're on your way to being small.' He tilts his drink. 'Look at those Chinese – they're super-rich guys, but they're not capitalists, they're on strings. And all those poor guys, working to live, and then they lift their heads, and there's riches – but it isn't Capital. It's choice – the Party guys. They choose.'

'I'm sure you're wrong,' I say.

'But you're not right either. Sitting there,' he says.

‘There’s reasons why you don’t dance and sing when going out to hunt,’ I say. Dan says,

‘Of course, there’s always reasons. Because the place is full of ghosts, live, dead. They have their special dance. Ghosts. Hunters. It is respect, not fear. This is the age of reasons, after all.’ I say,

‘It’s just I don’t see what kind of life comes from your head. Wherever you are at.’

Dan says, angrily, ‘There’s life. There are no different kinds. Nor different kinds of head. Do, don’t spy.’

I tell him, ‘My paper didn’t pay enough. I’m greedy so I took some more. And anything you write about that place, Kičevo, is true, and false, and no one cares.’

We’ve had enough of each other. I leave, and as I go, I see Dan move over to the lady in the aertex.

*

Back home. The road ends here, for some. For others, it’s just somewhere along. We’re all foreigners here, know it or not. These cheap rooms, was a hotel, but now those bones all filleted out, just places where you flop. Each for himself. You go in through a room full of the demented. Long-timers, live by the second. They see each of us enter, have forgotten us when we’ve crossed the room.

A guy, demented, quite normal-looking, rouses from the babble: 'Two girls were dancing in the road,' he says. 'A wind-up gramophone, dancing to the song "After the ball is over". I'll never forget them.'

'Well, you wouldn't,' I say.

'No one would,' he says.

'Do you remember anything else?' I ask. 'Anything at all?'

'How beautiful they were,' he says. 'All bound up in it. The scene.'

Memory, that useful thing ... and were there mountains, rowan trees? Folklore, or politics, to sharpen it all up?

'I mean, remember anything else at all,' I repeat.

'I dare say they were communists. Lots were those days.'

'Better not say, if you can't be sure,' I say.

'Soldiers?' he suggests.

'No,' I say. 'We're moving further away.'

*

Banging on my door: the girl from the bar.

'No, I know who you are, Fay, of course. Look, I'm not the dropping in on type.'

'I'm frightened to go back through the demented,' she says.

'No. No room. It's been hard, with Dan. Sex, jungles. Bringing everything down that's fallen anyway.'

'Well, then. Fuck you, I guess,' she says.

'Just one night, and only you,' I say.

'Who else do you see behind me?'

'Well, there could be Dan,' I say.

'It's you I'm asking.'

*

We watch a program about tower blocks in China.

I'm quite drunk.

I tell her, 'I write pieces for the papers.'

Fay says, 'Just bum around.'

'It's a responsible job,' I say, 'If you're caught out. What do you do?'

'This and that,' she says, 'But not bumming around.'

*

'Dan's an admirer of the Indians,' Fay says. 'He says they like Americans. Americans kill their enemies, right off if they don't torture them first, that is. No parleying. They love their children too. Dan says it lets you see the idea itself ...'

'Hohum,' I say. 'The idea itself. Sounds ominous.'

'The idea is, you can't choose your battles,' Fay says.

'Dan means the Indians have lost, so they can be trained up to another fight,' I say. The whole scheme has just become quite clear. The sex, children, fighting.

*

After many years, some arguments, some incoherent sex, here we are still, in a different place. I know nothing of her, Fay.

She says, 'This wanting to know people – it's a sickness. People are weird. That's all you need to know, and deeper down, the weirdness grows. The rest's excitement, the what you don't know and don't expect.'

If she makes money, I never see it. At least the aertex suit has gone.

*

Dan visits, and he says, 'My Indians? They fight. They bunch – it's quite disastrous. They'd be wiped out at once. That's brotherhood. And of course, it's hard for them, distinguishing one puffed up guy from all the rest: they can't assassinate.'

He asks Fay what she does, she says, 'I lobby. Some guy does something no one likes, and I call in, the radio, any media. I'm common sense, a public. Citizen zero, if you like. Quite reactionary at times. I defend the guy, whatever stupid thing he does. He pays me. But usually it's states, or cops. I trade a point of view.'

Dan says, 'Fay, that's quite corrupt.' She shrugs.

'You?' he asks me.

'I'm a source. I invent a story, it's denied, and then the guy you've lied about lays out his truth. It's media again.'

'Well,' says Dan, 'that sounds corrupt as well – but at least it's all about the truth.'

We stare at each other, maybe there is admiration there.

'You're rather carrion, you two,' says Dan laughing. 'Or maybe carrion crows.'

'Dan, you're rather smug,' I say.

'I'll pick you to the bone, if you want,' he says, laughing some more.

'Forget all that,' says Fay. 'All the bodies here are dead. The vultures too. We're all dead, our dead eyes looking at the sky.'

'Well,' says Dan, when he's out of Fay's embrace: 'You chose him, not me.'

'He had a room,' says Fay, seductively. She titillates, convention says it leads to something more. Unveiling. Even breakfast in a room, the two. But no – convention doesn't enter in.

Dan says, 'How'd you like I lead you from your grimy lives, and have you make some history, a name? Not just a name that someone gave, but something real, and earned, for making memories?'

'Oh yes,' I say, and do not think.

'Oh yes!' says Fay. She thinks, and says, 'Oh no! This guy here – gave me my freedom, hasn't got the force to keep me tied. These projects, Dan, with people all around – you enter as yourself, you never leave, you're broken and you crawl, and are not recognised.'

'Leave that out,' says Dan. 'The being recognised isn't what you want. It's being known . You see, all the success there is, requires a name. It's not the plot. It's heroes, maybe don't do things heroic – who cares? It's Crusoe and Karenina, and Pilgrim, Bolívar and Caesar, maybe somc awful guys who leave a mess, or don't do anything at all just like that whale, that Idiot, the Brothers, Molly Flinders – all of them, they make their space inside us all, like insects full of eggs. But – War and Peace? Well, those exist, but who remembers which was what?' He pauses, triumphant. He has started bad.

'Tell us, what enterprise you have in mind?' asks

Fay. 'Elections, finance, religion? Or more modern stuff. Dancing, maybe.' Dan says,

'I have some status with that group, those Indians, minority by any count—' and I interrupt,

'No, Dan, put minorities together and they're bigger than majorities. Besides, everyone is for your friends until the documentary ends – and then you see them, banging on your window, and the magic fades.' Dan says,

'No, no, I see I'll have to tell you in a different way. Those guys, the persecuted ones – they want their rights, and so they get them, and they disappear, they go into the mash. They want what everybody else already has, or thinks they've got. But – my guys have lost. For good. There's no one left for them to ask – and so ...'

There's heavy silence. He goes on,

'Intensity's the thing. Minorities is only numbers. What you want, is heat. Burning. The unassimilable.'

I say, 'Dan, I'm deeply disappointed, And you'd be somewhere, leading them?'

'Why, no,' he says, 'I plan to have an office. Several rooms. Agreeable.'

*

'I'm offering you something new,' says Dan. 'Not modern, and not retro. Not rich, not poor. Not humanist – we see where that has gone. No gods, no boss, and no heroes. Not quite real, and not quite not. You see these opposites, they wreathe around each other, they're a pair of snakes that hold each other's tail. If you are rich, there must be poor, and if you're rich, you must have more and more, else you're not really rich at all, you're nearly poor, and poor guys prod the grey and twiggy fields – and more and more of each ... And so it goes – you want your war – the guys will call for peace, you want some peace, and so your army grows immense and needs new stuff and rockets up to Mars and back again, perhaps—'

'Yes, yes,' says Fay. 'We know the world. We live here, just like you.'

'Of course, working things out – that's the hard one,' Dan says. 'There's Indians, there's maybe you two here, there's hosts up there,' and he waves to air and sky. 'Or it could be Fay alone. It's putting things together, making the new thing: ethereal State.'

I feel I must say something. 'I didn't start it off – truth, justice. Plots and interpretations. Things that are – but hard to pin them down. Like – how'd we get here, what's it for? It isn't even written down ...' and Fay interrupts,

'Oh yes it is! Of course it's written down. It's just you don't believe. You're in the business, that's what's wrong. I've seen you write – about Dan's Indians, "no massacres, just badly led, refusing generous terms ...'''

'And that's all true,' I say, 'There's always guys that looks for corpses when you write – if they don't find some, well, it's all the same. It's like Dan says – the jungle's full of pits and skulls. Who is to tell? There's always reasons, always something next, the scroll unrolls, and you can't roll it back, there's artists everywhere, their brushes full of coloured inks ...'

'Anyway,' says Dan, brushing history away, 'it's like the medievals: nothing certain, unpronounceable names, everything forged, romanticised, mistranslated. Then the moderns – science lasts a month or so, and all written over, more animals to kill, another little article to write. Think of those Indians, the crap matrimony with nature. Those guys are scared to death, a pebble in your shoe that wakes and eats your knee ...'

'They don't have shoes,' says Fay. 'That's why.'

'I don't want to check it out myself,' I say. 'We've screwed up reality, I've done my share in that, and so it's been for ever. Even writing down on paper – doesn't mean a lot,' and I feel wise, but wisdom brings despair, and so Dan says,

'Best just to forget. That's where it leads, you two. But – something new, I'd like to make, not written down, not cages full of mice. Not like those Vikings on your screen, young Fay, who take you to the underworld and promise you good sex ...'

'It's just my job,' she says, and shuts her little screen so he can't peep.

*

'Certainly,' says Fay, 'If I don't like you much, it means I could like someone else much much more.'

We've come to this airport, on the way to see Dan's Indians. 'It's not the wrong airport,' I say. 'It's the wrong country to start from.'

Important people come and go. 'It's hard to scintillate here,' says Fay, impatiently.

'Well, then,' I say. 'Stop sticking your icicle in my heart. It doesn't impress.'

'This place!' says Dan. 'Those planes – they make you think of death. Hovering over nothing. Like God, looking down and seeing plasticine.'

*

Dan reflects, 'Reality – yes, it's screwed up, but that's the way it's always been. No guidance has been given, ever.'

'Let's think of cheerful things!' says Fay. 'No one could write it down, so the reality – it's just a cabinet of curiosities. You wonder why a thing – a ghost, a twisted paw – is interesting to some collector and then you see the cabinet itself is full of holes and cages, dark eyes in the depths, all that.'

'That sounds a pointless trick to me,' I say. 'Besides, Fay's explanation does not explain a thing.'

The time will pass, it must. We wait. Then …

Some guy with a megaphone starts up: 'You guys, oh hear me. There's a difficulty for you, and we've your interests closely to our skin. There's massive flitting to and fro. Identity must surely be at risk – we know you cling to it, you hold it close, it's like your sex, your dad, your language, things you may believe or maybe not. In short – that's it for now! No more, the flights end for today, tomorrow we shall see ... Once lost, identity does not return, it's worse than crashing in the sea ...' and on he goes.

Fay says, 'What, what? Fog over China? Or bankruptcy, and we are penniless?'

'No, no,' Dan says. 'Calm, now. It's to preserve identity. And that is right, we cling to it,' but Fay shouts, 'My case! I cling to that.'

Dan says her case is hopeless, and we laugh; she cries. She says,

'I wanted to eat caterpillars. Now, I've lost my pyjamas.'

'Rejoice!' I say. 'You never outguess experience!' and she says,

'Yes, you can, you suck it in. How could you believe it just arrives?'

'Well,' says Dan, 'where can we go? It seems we can't go anywhere, or else we lose identity ...'

'Hush,' I say. 'Experience comes, let's say we suck

it in like grubs, or else it falls on you, quite like a python, falling from a tree. What matters is desire, like wanting to see those Indians, and how they fit Dan's plan.'

But Dan is wandering off, he shouts to us, 'Forget the Indians – now they've lost, they live in camps, maybe in tiny houses like they give to losers everywhere, so tight, one room.'

We feel we've been invited to go outside and wander round the fields. 'Some guy said we're being rocketed,' says Fay, and Dan is angry:

'Forget it, Fay. Here you see no pieces of artillery. All is tranquil and besides, fuck the suitcase, any traveller knows you have to leave it all behind. Nostalgia! Poison.'

'Well, yes, ok,' says Fay. 'It was a special thing, you know – but if we're travelling—'

'As any traveller knows, dear Fay, travel is in the mind, and that alone,' Dan says. 'I'm getting close to it, the something new to stack up on the old, like pictures overpainted. Over, over. The new idea. It's just – those Indians, if they're in houses, I'll need to send a trumpeter to wake them up.'

'Tell us, Dan, tell us, and have done.'

'Hmmm,' he says, not being rushed. 'There's one big chief I know, that's bunkered down and safe, New York, or somewhere like. I'd introduce him ...' I lose patience, and I threaten him. He says,

'We shall enrol our citizens. Then we found our

State. There's lots of electronic guys, who seek their fortunes on the net, and wisdom too. The net! Our lusty fish!'

I say, 'That's nonsense, Dan. Those guys sign up to anything, they think that what they think this hour is angel plumes,' and then he turns on me,

'No, no! You have to make them sweat. Each day – trick questions, just like in real States.'

'Pure chance,' says Fay. 'They answer randomly, just like in real States.'

Patiently, Dan says, 'You miss the point. They give me all their cash. I'm their trustee. The answer right and wrong – it costs. Just like the real. With that we buy some justice, and some truth.'

I'm bored. I say, 'You're just like all that awful crew that wants to make us pay for dawns, and sunsets too. They price you, and their Death, dear Dan. You're just a pile of ash, cut-price. You may believe your Indians are real, and soldiers too, enforcing stuff – but in the end, it's just like all the rest, your State Ethereal. All states start off as good guys, just like yours ...' and Fay says,

'The State – it's an idea. So, Dan, what's yours? What's your Idea?'

'Well, now,' says Dan, 'let's walk some way along this road, and as we stroll, I'll have it come to me. The Idea that founds it all.'

*

'We've walked a way already now,' says Dan. 'Poor people, rich ones, powerful, all of that – we agree, there's nothing particular we can do about them all. Many are, no doubt,' and he pinches my arm, 'awful people. The principle must be – "from each according".'

'I don't remember any agreeing about that,' says Fay, 'but no doubt, sadly, it is so.'

'You two,' says Dan, brightening, 'must have your portraits done. We'll be three brisk startled images. Three, with a gender mix, is good. It's a compromise – with monotheism, but not quite promiscuous, nor cosy. That will do for religion – lots of it, of course. Property, on the other hand – so far, we have none. Cash we do need, and I've explained how that's available. But not for follies, and in any case, what, what do we want to buy? Vanity, that's sheer vanity,' and Fay trembles when she hears 'case' and 'vanity', but does not interject.

Dan stares at us, aligns a thumb, a blade of wheat, as if he's launching in some painting. 'My!' he says, 'Fay! You're so beaky and so bony. What can we do with you?'

He makes a mock of me, sags down his jaw and cheeks: 'Quite the Windbeutel there!' he says: 'I love those buns from Austria – the cream: echt Schlag!

How you must enjoy them, by the barrowload. The windbag. That fits you well, and we must make that do.'

Fay says, 'Dan, it's maybe better you explode your plan yourself, than have us laugh at you behind your back. Though, I admit, I always wanted to be a State – the marching, and the praying. It's hard to resist all that.'

'No, no,' says Dan. 'I'm wholly serious. We have the fields of music and of architecture. That's our resource, the maths as well. Now socialism has fallen down, and capitalism too – that's dealt with that! Onward we go,' and so we do, a walking slow.

Without the aeroplanes, the sky is quiet, unnaturally. Fay says, 'Look, there's a malibu. It's come a long long way.'

'And so have we,' I say. 'We've walked all round the airport, useless its lying here.'

'No, no,' says Dan again. 'It's not for money, the Indians will fight to right the wrongs – just like we fought for them. They'll be paid well, just like we were. But remember this, we must accept no task we can't accomplish – otherwise, what idiots we'd seem! What we want is what we have. And, Fay, do you really think to buy that stuff that's on display? Those little airport booths?'

She shakes her head, no, no. 'Of course!' she says, and,

'I want to see those Indians. That's what our

ticket's for.'

'They've changed, those Indians,' says Dan. 'Even as we've walked around. It's been a useful stroll, around, around, three times around ...'

We went round once – and still we do not understand. Dan stole our images. Fay said – that suitcase, saw it in a store, openwork, metallic – a sculpture, surely it was Dan said to bring it, personal things tied in ...

'It's better for those malibus,' says Dan. 'There's no more planes. They're sucked inside, the storks, and that is bad for everyone,' and that is one thing true, the runways full of storks like torn-up newspapers, they squat and groom, and strut on broken tripod legs. He says, 'Those portraits look more real than you. We needed something quite authentic and to capture you, it only takes a blink. That's how it is with pictures – you can live in them, they're all interiors, some have music in them too. Whether they are blurs, like when you wake, or lines of shelves and fridges in the dark – it gives a sense of something caught and fixed, you see a solid thing when all the rest is moving on ...'

Fay says, 'Why there aren't planes – can we believe the explanation?'

'Well,' I say. 'No doubt there's lots of reasons given, and it's certain that the guys that work there, they get tired of all those people, tears and cases, the losses, the planes go off – do they return? I doubt it.'

'Enough of guesses, the deal was I'd take you from

corrupting tasks and make you clean,' says Dan.

'Dan thinks he can be saved, and as a favour save us too,' says Fay, who's taking heart again: 'It's not I'm vain, it's just I cling to things,' and that we know is true.

'Let's go see that guy,' says Dan. 'Those Indians, if we get to see – they don't enjoy the violence, but they do like pleasing me. That makes them model citizens by any measure, models for the better State,' but I notice there is something in his eye, a lack, a disconnect they call it, some missing piece, a bridge without a middle span. He says, 'Ah well, you start off from both shores, the joining up is hard, from where you were to where you want to go, but bridges in the end are always built.'

*

We go to see his friend. His contact, maybe he's a partner, with his portrait somewhere too. The door is marked 'Hail to the chief!'

'I told you so,' says Dan, and we're convinced. The bunker has a door that's thicker than a safe's.

'Yes,' says the guy. 'It's true that I do banking too. So if you've any cash, just lay it out, some guy will count it, tuck it dark and cool away.'

The guy has eyes so blue, he maybe got the colour

from a parrot's tail, his hair is black as forest roots. Fay says to me,

'For sure, this guy is crooked,' and I say, 'Hush, Fay, in this part of town the guys all look like this,' and then he takes us down some steps, and there's an Indian village – guys spearing fish, the gals are grinding breakfast on their thighs, and little kids are running round and doing useless things.

'These powerful guys all have a village buried somewhere down beneath,' says Dan.

It sounds like an excuse. For what? Fay and I, we make no sound. We watch the villagers, they don't watch us, they just accumulate some food.

Later, Fay says, 'Dan's preparing something quite magnificent. And then, the end. He cares lots about that stuff, and I don't care at all.'

I say, 'Fay, you must tell me what and when. We're close, I thought, an average, a couple. After all, I took you in. It was a favour,' and she says,

'Dan's suggestion. Because you're weak, is all.'

I say, 'It was part of someone's plan. I thought it mine. It seems it wasn't so.'

'Plan? Plan?' Fay laughs, 'I didn't know that anyone could have a plan.'

I say, 'I've always been for you, you guys. Women.'

Fay laughs again: 'I hear your dry brain rattling in its shell. You think, you think. It's sad. Old thoughts.'

Dan joins us, and he says, 'Too bad about that case.

It's gone, I fear, though I've no doubt it will turn up. But – us ... how hard it was to get here: how and where should we return?'

I ask Fay, 'What's so special about your case? The extra special, I might say.'

'The metal flowers. All sculpted. Special for travelling with.'

'You mean, it's platinum,' I say.

'That's what Dan says,' says Fay. 'That, and my personal things.'

'We must look for that suitcase. The platinum one,' says Dan.

'Yes,' I say. 'I'd not forgotten which one.'

This is a bus station, and we sprawl on the wooden benches. Fay gives me a piece of newspaper. You can read '-blatt'.

'There!' she says. 'That means leaf. You can put it over you, and you're in the forest. Waiting for princesses.'

Birch trees as far as you can see, so far far off until they make a grey wall. I say,

'It means roach too. This place is famous for them.'

'That's what you get under leaves,' says Fay briskly.

She and Dan move away.

I'm tired of watching them.

They do not come back.

*

'Can you give me a ticket to Memphis?' I ask. 'My money doesn't seem to work.' The clerk asks,

'Which Memphis? We don't go to any of them. We'll take your money now – it's suspended, it'll come back fresh and clean, you'll see.'

He says to a colleague, 'This guy, seems dumped, abandoned. Give him comfort, there's a love.'

His colleague wears a uniform, not a dumpy one, but like a Japanese schoolgirl's. Banish the thoughts – this is not the culture ... She says,

'Yes, your friends, so tall and proud. The woman, like a model, beak like a prow, full of improvisations, and him – overflowing with a destiny, like that couple from French poetry. At school ...' I interrupt,

'In my mind they're quite runty. It depends, of course, what is the average.'

'No, no,' she says. 'Quite noble. No wonder they wanted off and be alone.'

Her badge says 'Apple' – I guess she redirects lost people. With a bite comes wisdom.

'I'm not lost,' I say. 'It's them who's lost, my company.'

Apple says, 'Well, we'll take you home, me and Gus, the ticket guy. Just for one night. And no one else.'

'I'd sooner wait here for my friends,' I say.

She laughs. 'No, it's my job, this charity. Your friends, all friends, they don't come back.'

'And when I've slept?' I ask.

'We bury you in the garden. What d'you think, we'd just dump your body out?' I don't enter her game, entering the spirit, it is called. She goes on,

'We're both sergeants, Gus and I. That means that we can have a plan. Leave this place, for one.'

I wonder if there's Indians in their basement too. Well, here's their place, and yes, it's tall, it shakes, cement is turning back to shingle and salt waves. There in the basement there's a slice of everyone, Colombians, real Indians, pounding maize and roots. Up, up we climb, no elevator, up a mountain, just to sleep and pass the dark.

Apple says, 'Your friends are crap – we'll set you up with more, then on your way. Here everyone assimilates like mercury. It's all discovery, first times. Columbus comes and goes like on a loop.'

Gus shows, he's home, he throws his pistol down: he says to Apple, 'How's the plan today?'

He says the plan is – go down south where buses do not go: – with cowboys riding up and down, a herd of Charolais, and other guys who rise at dawn and do the work.

Then Apple sets down a lot of cans and says we either choose one, eat direct, or throw it all together ... there's a feast, and then we lie to sleep on mats, as 'That's the healthy way,' says Apple.

And she crawls on mine, and whispers, Gus has Inuit blood, he read it in a book, what comes now is hospitality, besides, 'It is my job,' she says. 'It's agape, not eros,' but I do not read the books which tell you which is which, but sex with Apple's part of literature, a jolt you get like joining cables with bare hands ... and on and on, and all the night, the details all set out, not one is missed....and at the end you never need another night like that, it clings, it bonds with you, it's down in memory and stored, and then I ask,

'Do all abandoned guys get this? I'm not an Inuit myself,' and Apple says that guys who're dumped, or simple hoboes – there is no prejudice, it is her job, and anyway, the ticketing Gus does has numbed him, but love is all around, like in the literature, and those that have a plan are into answers, not the questions that are unanswerable. And Apple is unanswerable too, and when I think of Fay and Dan, those two crabbed fruits, their intellects quite soured by scheming and by moving on, well, Gus and Apple seem the genuine thing. '*Echt Schlag!*' I say, as from a sack they bring the pastries out, flown in or bussed, I'm sure, from Austria, and fresh that day.

'Eat, eat,' says Apple, rosy as the dawn, and Gus says, 'Yes, and when you're done, a little favour's all we ask.'

'Oh no!' I say. 'You filmed it all and we must do retakes ...'

'No, no,' says Gus. 'I've been in libraries where

there's padlocked shelves with stuff like what young Apple does. It's literature, for sure, but all we want is just a coupla lines to say that Apple knows her job, and give it to the boss, and get promoted. Then we buy the Charolais ...' and on he goes. I say,

'It's true that I'm a guy that writes for papers, all that stuff, that's nearly dead. But what I write – they say it's make-believe. Truth and wisdom yes, those I have. It's just what Apple did is all the same, and all those chained-up books – they say the same.'

'OK,' says Gus. 'A wise guy, and truthful too. A coupla lines you'll not refuse. It's make-believe, but it brings cash, and more than you can make each year,' and that is true, no doubt. I sign the letter with an Inuit name, quite unpronounceable.

It works, and Apple's made a captain, and they buy the Charolais, we start off trekking down, all three we're following the beasts, shouting words we find in nature to encourage them – quite untranscribable.

*

I say, 'Emotions, Apple, that's what people want to see. To stimulate their own.'

We've got to where we want to be, and so we're free to meditate, without involvement, life is process, no more hooves to keep in view.

'Emotions? I am full of them,' she says. 'And when we've ate the Charolais, there'll be still more emotion left.'

For we are farmers now. I look out across the hills that roll, the lilting trees, the clouds that swoop and leap, and round and round they race and fill the sky ...

'It's the hunger,' says Gus. 'The tilted landscape. Churns it all up. The consciousness.'

'We've fulfilled our plan,' says Apple. 'On to the next, I guess.'

I think of Fay, onward she drives, no compass, head turned to the waves, Dan on her deck, heaving at wet sails. I say to Gus, 'We should look for permanence. These cows are very limited as food, as future too.'

*

We eat the last of the cows, and look out on the land we leave tomorrow. Apple says,

'The thing magnificent Fay wants, and Dan as well, maybe – I'm not so sure about. My family once was part of some magnificence, their bones went into it.'

I don't know what to say, for sure it's all been said before. Gus says,

'We Inuits – we've never taken part in this magnificence. That is a line, a boundary, we've never crossed. And as for Apple, all this goddam stuff, the stories, families ...'

She says, 'They thought we'd all be better off with names like Rose and Petal – names that don't arouse some folk.'

Gus is angry again, he says, goddam, just do the job, give pleasure if you can and spare the pain for animals, if you must, for after all, they're part of you, that's in the book he's read. But Apple's story strikes a splintered note. We bring our mats outside, and stare up at the stars.

'I thought I'd rejoice when it all fell down,' says Gus, 'but it fell on me. And then I thought of all the years to come, of struggling, building something that I'd never see its shape. Job, cash, everything. More struggle,' and he looks quite sad, and Apple says,

'Just think – some people, somewhere, must be doing well.' Gus shrugs.

I say, 'You Inuits – you've done quite good – just find your things to eat and wear, then sit around and sing.'

Gus looks sadder still. 'It's difficult,' he says. 'We can't all go and live on snow, and dangle through the ice, and hope.'

'There's nothing to be done,' I say. 'You need to find rich guys who want your bundle full of gold,' and they both laugh, and that is comradeship, we understand, there's nothing to be done, no one to call.

*

Back in the bus station, here we are, we sprawl along the wooden benches. Apple says,

'It's healthy, so.'

I say, 'You can't expect to get your jobs back?' They are quiet, so then I say,

'We ate your dreams.'

'Beef!' says Gus.

'Yes, beef,' says Apple dreamily. 'So much we vomited.'

I ask, 'Our money's valueless again? The first time – how did we react? With protest, or nobility?'

I see that 'beef' is on their lips. I don't insist.

*

Two runty types are circling round. I think, 'A moustache and a baseball cap, that guarantees anonymity complete.'

It's Fay and Dan. Fay says,

'Where you been? We just stepped out.'

A long first step, a month, a year. I ask,

'And did you find the case?'

'It's close, it's close,' says Dan. 'The system's cracking up more often now, it's best you're into platinum. Those malibu – there's was smart birds. You need to find a destination, trim your expectations, if you had them.'

We meditate on this, and then Fay asks, 'Who's these weird guys attached, relaxed?'

She points at Apple and at Gus. They lie like seals, and glisten, full of hope.

We cling, we calculate – better to be one, or three, or five? And what is best to be, follow the good life, or settle down in what we have?

'We need,' says Gus, 'A different history, a different place from which to start, and finish too.'

'There is my plan,' says Fay. 'We don't know each other – but then, knowing and liking are quite some different things.'

'That's not worth bringing up,' says Gus, and I say,

'One death can't represent the death of all,' and Apple says it does if it is you. I say,

'Apple, you gave me an experience ... I don't need any more. And no repeats.'

Fay says that sounds a terrible thing, whatever it might be. Apple says,

'I gave you nothing. Look! I'm here and quite integral. The experience is yours, you take it, do as you like with it – and no repeats.'

No buses leave from here, but there is oil around, the air, the ground, the sound of horns and trumpets as they made their way, like elephants in triumph.

Dan shrugs, and says, 'You guys can pass your days

and waste away ... those last guys saying 'hi!' to Gus and going home. His comrades. It was desolation at the start – that doesn't mean that's how it ends.'

'That's true,' says Fay. 'But not worth bringing up.'

Apple says it's like in jail, or on a pilgrimage – we each should tell a tale, one that reveals: more than the crime, more than the quest.

Fay says, 'It sounds a little precious, and besides, there's some of us that makes a living make-believing,' and Apple says the truth is not at stake – in jail or on a pilgrimage – you go for revelation, not for truth, that's been decided somewhere else.

'It might be fun,' says Dan, but says it with a sombre laugh, and Gus is bright, he says that Inuit, they live on stories, there's the simple life, there's not much else to do, nature gives the little that you need, no cash, no capital, no movies, and no buses. Nor no bosses. After that, we see dark corners glitter, there are stairs – a wonder and delight ... and Dan says if Gus is an Inuit, he should catch some food, for all of us. Apple says, that if she could, she'd fly us, all of us, away from here, and Fay asks, 'To an airport?' and she scoffs. Gus says we're stereotyping, and he chose his group in preparation for the worst: 'The melt, the water, no green thing that shoots and flowers. Where there was white, there's nothing now – you shed your clothes and float, there's just the sky ...'

'That's not your story, Gus,' says Fay. 'And let's not hear the one about the blind hunters and the walrus. I'll start us off,' and Dan cuffs her round the head in fun, and says, 'Do tell about what you did before you leeched on us.' Fay says,

'It's all to do with resurrection and that cat. They sent it in a box to Mars, it's dead up there but still alive down here. That's where your science meets religion – not transport by aliens, just boxes sent with bodies in that's living there and buried here,' and Apple says,

'No, Fay, my dear. You've got the story wholly wrong. Besides, it's hearsay, not a thing that's part of you,' and Fay says that's the point, her life's been hard, but cats can have it worse, and Gus says there's no milk on Mars, that animal is good as dead on landing there. Apple says you must believe in aliens and religion, the people say the Inuit and the Indians are aliens left when their ships broke down, and can't adapt, assimilate, besides, you can't just disbelieve in everything, and Dan says better to believe in things that do you harm, like ants and jiggers.

'No, no,' shouts Gus. 'You guys have got it wrong! It's the bourgeoisie! They want these tales of eating cows, incest and hunger, like we guys here have known from very young. And Fay! it's fantasy you tell, some miracle to lift us up, a false messiah cat ... Dread, terror. Dan tells that to keep the guys away, and pious too, while you stalk through your wilderness ... Magnificence! It's only you, and your imagining – you conquer jungles: jungles they remain, and you're remote, untouchable, the hero of the scrabbling life.

All to admire you, but there's nothing there, you bring back just a travellers' tale of tribes that's happy eating crap and singing songs...' and on he goes.

'Well, Gus,' asks Fay, 'What is your tale?'

'The guys and gals that drive the bus – and sit out there in front – yes, they sing songs that no one hears, and drive through banks of snow and spume, and bandits! – walls of rock and tentacles that try the doors, they're round your throat. But on you go. That's courage, and the destination ...'

'Another depot, I expect,' says Dan briskly. 'So, Gus was a driver, got through safe, maybe his passengers as well. And Fay, her mystery outside the pub and round the corner, passions suspended, "just some drinks", a chat, a kind of agency that never strikes a deal ...'

*

'You can't hear the money falling down,' says Fay, 'But those grand buildings – wow!' She turns to me. 'Now, it's your turn, your story.'

'I don't need to have one,' I say. 'I'm just the joint of union, without me, you lot would not have held together, looking out on desolation. And besides, it was me suggested we all move our birthday to the same day – that way there's destiny and no coincidence. It makes the presents easier, and remembering,' and Gus agrees, his book says that's what Inuit do, and socialists no doubt, and Apple says it was her story that was due, and Fay says,

'Apple, you must tell us something new, not just piling other people's stories up,' and Apple says that's how it's done, but how, when she was small, her mother hid her in a hole beneath a tree – the father killer, neighbours too, poverty that made them lick the paint off doors, all that, religion too, no doubt, and she was raised...

'No! Not by squirrels?' Dan is laughing. Apple goes on, 'I thought that only God told stories, and I hadn't one. Then people came and took the others all away, and other people, came and bought me. That is all.'

'No, Apple, not all,' I tell her. 'People like you – you draw the others out,' and she says, well, that must be chance, she says she's troubled that the others make a guess about their future lives, a game you're made to play, and she sees only trees, the birch trees, shoulder to shoulder, dwindling far away, like the tsar's army, till they make a wall, that's grey, like distant purple left discolouring in the sun ... and that is how I see my future life, she says. I say,

'Yes, Apple, I can see it too, that is my life, exactly,' and she says,

'It may be everyone's – the point is, you're not there, it doesn't mean a thing, and we are separate, and lying on the mat and having dreams ...' and then Dan interrupts and says that dreams are just the peelings and the pips, how he was born in mansions, tiny ponies drew him round the park in lacquered carts, and servants brushed his teeth, the brushes made of hair from pumas' tails.

'Then why go off exploring?' Apple asks. She doesn't quite believe.

'It left me with the sense,' says Dan. 'That I'm immortal. Not only that – invincible as well,' and Gus says heroes of that kind don't figure in his book, you're guided by the stars, and as you stare – there! that crack you didn't see ... down through the ice you go, it's red and thick, the water there, like jelly at a party, you can't suck it in, and far above are all your kin, they're gesturing and making magic signs, it does no good, you're stuck into the thickness, you can't speak or breathe – and Fay says,

'Jelly! That is all? Kid's food for heroes – though I admit, some luxury is what I need,' and she and Apple pinch and punch, and I climb on the girders and look down. I dangle like a puma, and they're squabbling and breaking up the benches. Apple shouts at Fay,

'You tiny giant – too tall to be a decent dwarf!' and Fay says Apple's body's cut out with a spade from compost, and they shout on, and Dan and Gus – they slug it out, until I cry.

'Stop! Stop! Here's Mr Silverside! His is the scheme that sets us free!' and there he stands, his sharkskin suit is splendid, and that leather trilby, shiny black – gleams like a helm. It's true he's rather old and frail, he staggers with his weight, his cargo stowed some generations back, the bundles packed in leaves that's sprouting out, grey and unfragrant, and he says,

'You homeless guys should go where all the others went. The huts is right for you.'

He snaps his cane about, beheading absent dandelions: 'Here, you won't see, for instance – the recovery. You'll hear the buildings coming down. They're pointed down, their heads, down, down, into the ground. You notice how it smells in here,' and he pauses, but we've noticed scarcely anything. Our stories have been told, but why we are the things we are, we cannot tell ... 'Below the ground,' says Mr Silverside, 'it's clean. Of course,' he says to Apple, who has wrinkled up her nose. 'There's lights.'

We're unimpressed. Fay says, 'We do well here, we're eating out these vending machines – you fix the box inside so that the cash is on a loop,' and Mr Silverside says he knows all that: 'I see in time you'll realise, there is a flaw ...'

Dan says, recovery or not, there should be walking on the land, and herding stuff to eat up here, and Silverside says, 'Well, out there it's capitalism still, of course. You idiots – did you expect a change? In the huts, though, no sleeping mats required – there's beds for each, and sleep is guaranteed. The question is – and I can help with this – if you could go, where would it be?'

Fay says, 'If I knew where I wanted to be, I'd be there,' and Dan agrees, and Dan says we've not missed out the future, if that is what it is, outside, it's just the reel of rise and fall ... it's just we've called a halt, a rest. Apple says,

'We've done the farming, and Gus knows all about the fish,' and Mr Silverside says that is good, and we could grow some mushrooms here. It seems a meagre thing to do, to spend a unique life to watch them grow. So Mr Silverside's amused, he says we've big ideas, and Apple says, despite appearances, we are all big to match, each knows what the others did: Magnificence, transform the scene, all that has been, will be again.

'Of course,' says Mr Silverside. 'I must help you find that case. Though I don't see you helping anyone – or even knowing they exist.'

'You mean,' says Fay, pretending shock, 'going into prisons, such?'

'Here, we don't oppress, and aren't oppressed,' says Apple primly.

At first, I think that Silverside's an evil man, and then, that he might just as well be good, or just all right. Then I, or one of us, must be the evil one ... but to be that, you must perform some monstrous deed, at least concur ...

Apple says, 'Evil comes by doing properly your job, and making contracts. The evil: doing nothing that's so bad, you let the humans think the monstrous things and do them ... you draw the consequence, that's all.'

I'm not appeased. I say, 'The consequence must be laid down and understood, or else it's free-for-all ...'

Mr Silverside says, 'I can't be a leader – you're not quite free for me to lead you.'

'That's no loss,' says Fay.

I say, 'You mean, we can't leave? This crap choice we made – we can't get out?'

'You can leave, but under terms. Under indictment, as it were,' says Mr Silverside.

'Here, we can't do anything,' Apple could cry, and I could too.

'You could worship your ancestors,' says Silverside roughly, 'or become them. Everything turns out, in time.'

'No, we can't,' says Apple. 'We don't know who they are.'

'It comes with the wind,' says Mr Silverside. 'And sweeps you quite away. At the last, everyone understands.'

'What's the crime supposed to be?' asks Dan, 'Lying?'

Mr Silverside cocks his small head, uncommitting. Fay says,

'That seems a tiny thing.'

Mr Silverside says firmly, 'No! Make-believing when we have the truth before us – no, that's not a trivial thing.'

Fay insists, 'It's newspapers! It's airy talk! It doesn't count. Science, religion, reality – those are stuck out there, a truth is tied to each, like mock fruit on a tree.'

'Well,' says Mr Silverside, 'You wanted me to tell, say why you can't leave. I've told you – the truth.'

'But who?' asks Dan.

'No one in particular,' says Mr Silverside. 'Don't personalise. Truth, justice – that's not someone's guess. You had your fun. Now, pay!...' and Dan interrupts,

'If we had the suitcase, maybe that could sort it out?

'No, no,' says Silverside, 'You're very poor at wheedling. That case, a metal sculpture, no more. What did you think – a quiddity? Your values, each and individually?'

'It all seems casuistry,' says Fay, recovering.

'It is, it is,' says Mr Silverside. 'The beauty lies in that. You guys – you didn't work. You ate. Lots. Now, you have to pay it back. That is morality, and ethics too.'

'There's nothing here to do,' says Gus patiently. 'You see, the buses left. Newspapers too.'

'I'll leave you to puzzle out,' says Mr Silverside. 'Of course, you won't reach any absolutes. But just think on ... Think of Montaigne. Lucretius. It's all there, and elsewhere besides.' He laughs, and I see he draws the depot's doors closed behind him, they're magnificent, chased with scenes of hunt and victory.

These doors – closed. Is it War? Or Peace? I can't remember. Maybe the war's outside. Here there is peace – we shall accommodate.

It's Apple on the girders now, she swoops and dives, that body confident, a river friendly with the mountain and the sea. She makes us think of apricots, of hovering things. She sings, she shouts. Ah yes, that body, better than a dream – and as she loops and wheels, a breeze, leaves from Madagascar, sweet and medicinal ...

Dan walks. Machete on his shoulder, one eye grounded, the other after pythons in the trees. 'I walk and walk,' he says. 'And nothing's in my way. So, you can walk for ever,' and it's true, or nearly so.

Fay says to me, 'When we left you, we went as far away as possible. Dan and I, we made love by the river. As I always wanted. It was an end, but nothing ended,' and I'm put out. I say,

'Yes, Fay, but for a year?'

'Oh,' she says. 'It was that long? Only that?'

Are we seeking truth – or a trick – to let us out? It's all unlikely – people all around are making freedom on the streets, they say, maybe there is truth out there, waiting to be found, like chocolate eggs, hidden in the garden. Maybe we'd better do our time, not fret. Find something else to do, more do-able, unpicking ropes, or tunnelling.

Before he left, Mr Silverside said, 'Of course, we take responsibility – the vending machines, we'll keep them filled.'

They are not always full.

I say to Gus, 'Your identity. It seems quite spurious.'

'Well,' he says. 'You think it all comes from your granny, or a book.'

'Yes,' I say. 'It is a make-believe, especially in your case. You sell tickets, going to nowhere. That's what you are, and there's an end.'

Gus says, 'Even you must see that's crap. Try to find out how things work through.' He must be right. I say,

'I didn't know.' I persist. I say, 'Apple's the only one of us that's doing anything.' Gus is irritated, and he says, 'Apple isn't doing anything, she's being.'

I say to Fay, 'I didn't know you followed your emotions so. It causes disappointment ...' and she's irritated too, and says,

'It was a phase. It leaves no sign. That's how the best things go,' and Dan is walking up and down, watching for insects, on him it didn't leave a sign – the passion.

Mr Silverside appears, he says: 'You know, I am protecting you outside from ... well, all the usual things you can't do much about. This here is not a prison, brings me no joy.'

I say, 'It's an experiment, then? That makes it all right. Now, let me guess – the women, they're the ones deciding, but it's Gus who tells the stories, Dan who wanders off the track. My! – he's afraid, there's nothing good he finds, but on he goes, conquering a thing inside, maybe ... And what will set us free? Why – it's the case! A banal thing, for sure. With Fay's old clothes inside, but nonetheless, maybe the key that lets us out, and there is new around.'

Well, Mr Silverside, I see the key is his, he's said the outside works as it has always done ... He says,

'No, no, not an experiment, a *mise en scène*. And look, you've guessed it, dirtied up the scheme. I've just a key to let you out – no code! A code's beyond me, much too scholarly. I'm not that type.'

*

Apple says, 'We took you to Memphis – it seemed like you wanted.'

I say, 'Music and pyramids! – instead, treading along in all that stuff.'

She says, 'That's the way cows are. Now, if you want, you could get out. There's always a door, unlocked or only jammed.'

I say, 'No, Apple, it's direct experience I'm after. Making a good choice for once.'

She says it's gamblers always make the wrong decision, the thing is, to make the book: 'You could try a glide up here,' she says.

‘No, no,’ I say. ‘I lie upon the girders, I don’t stand and leap around. And if I fall, I’d want that you should catch me.’

‘I wouldn’t bet on that,’ she says. ‘You take the risk, like all the rest.’

Dan and Gus are watching the videos, and we hear ‘oh no’ and ‘wow’. It’s bus wrecks. Gus says, ‘Some guys do politics – that’s what it’s like,’ and Dan says the jungle’s full of it, wrecks and politics, and Fay says they’re reactionary, both of them, the temptation is always there, a change so great you can’t imagine it, or just some details – and there’s Apple, hanging upside down, and promising us nighttimes of bodies if we catch her, if she falls, and Fay says we wouldn’t know if she is falling till she hits, we’ve not been trained for quick reactions ... It’s like where Gus says he’s from, they move so slow, the things are slowly massive, ice and bears.

*

Fay says, ‘Those demented, long ago ... it’s horror I should feel, but such a desire too – making some sense. Like – “after the ball” ....’

‘No, you idiot,’ shouts Dan. ‘How’d you come to make sense if you don’t know what of?’

‘Sense, I said, not remembrance,’ says Fay. ‘Dan,

you're obsessed.'

'So what?' asks Dan. 'That is where the sense lies.'

*

Some say that Icarus didn't make a sound, as he came down. At least he had his wings. Some paint him mute, some – with mouth agape. It all depends, what kind of paint you use.

Apple – she has no wings, but down she comes – so swift, and lies there, like a swift that's hit a perpendicular, they've nothing but a tiny stubborn head, sharp semi-disc of wings, and claws. She's come right down. 'Too good to live,' says Gus, who cries. It sounds a note anomalous. The rest are torn between a tear, and fear and outrage.

Too late for anything – 'Reactions are banal,' says Dan, 'but gymnasts – what can we say they leave behind?'

Fay says with our memories we should write down a line or two, an epitaph – 'Here's one, it's not quite apt – "Her nightingales live on." That's my proposal,' and we all agree, it has the Greek, that angle, and the chime with Icarus ...

'On the other hand,' says Dan, 'she didn't leave a thing, still less a poem or inscription, not a gene, an anecdote,' and there's a sound, a voice that comes from out the tomb –

'Oh no,' says Apple's voice. 'I slipped,' and so we understand – she'd have been missed, although it seems we'd nothing left from her, and Apple says her referent's the swift – but maybe nightingale, on some low bough, is best.

'She was the only one who told the truth,' says Mr Silverside. 'Though the results from that are small,' and Dan says, 'That's contested too,' and Apple says she hurts, and that is likely true.

*

'You brought in this guy, Mr Silverlake,' Dan shouts at me: 'Who's behind him? Is he an emissary? Leading us out, keeping us in? Both?'

Fay starts to hit me, 'Spy, spy!' she shouts.

Dan says, 'Fay can be quite sweet, you know. When she's asleep ...' I say,

'I thought, someone to stir us up ...' and Mr Silverside says,

'Hey! You true communists! You're not popular outside. It isn't really clear if you are good or bad. Apple, now, she's clumsy – but Gus and Dan, minorities, these treks they do, recruiting – and Fay ...'

'Fay is quite beautiful,' says Dan. 'When in repose. You cannot read a thing that's bubbling inside, it could be vacant shell. And when she wakes, it's clear, she's travelled in her sleep, we don't know where, and she won't tell. Again, it might be something cogitated, a web of ponderings ...'

'It's true,' says Silverside. 'Transgression isn't easy now, things fall down by themselves, it might seem blaming you, or anyone, for anything at all – is just a way to shift attention from here to there. But you'll agree – it's justice, must be done to everyone.'

'Outside they may be hostile,' I say.

Dan says, 'I'm not scared of that – or, best to say, I'm very scared, and that's the way that serves.'

Mr Silverside looks us over: 'You don't seem very grown up,' he says. 'But that will have to do.'

Fay scowls at me, says how I've always wanted this – to draw us in, then lead us out. Gus says,

'Goddam, yes! A house – that's got a door you open and you close, just when you like.'

'We'll tell at once,' says Fay. 'The truth about the place outside. This stuff about the truth is mostly crap. Sometimes it's clear, not complicated, quite easy,' and we're excited by it all, a little terrified.

*

We find a little door. I lead them out. Far far behind is Mr Silverside. Victory? Defeat? Recovery?

*

Apple turns, looks back and says, 'That building's absolutely indifferent,' our bus depot – as if that's her discovery. We press on, in the streets there's crowds of young, some with beards, and some without. The buildings here are big and high, 'That's where we made our money – look, they're at it now!' says Fay, and guys are selling little pokes of stuff to eat.

There's music, very loud, but in the open, obviously, the sound – it has no tail, it's loud but thin, two instruments, jacked up, there is no hook to cling to you.

'It's like it was before,' says Fay. 'All.'

Some signs flash up and down. Allelujah, they say.

Dan says, 'We need to find the history that's under this. Until we do, we don't know if we're in or out.'

'Oh no,' shouts Fay. 'Look, look – we're weird!' We stare – there we are, reflected in some glass.

I say, 'It's because we're bunched along,' but if we had that suitcase we'd look weirder still, and not know if it's a thing that others steal, or if it looks as if we've found or stolen it. There's guys in uniform, but if they're cops, or just on leave, we cannot tell.

'Come on!' I say to Apple, who is skipping, dipping, strengthening her knees. 'We just dropped out a while, it's all exactly as it was before,' and Dan says 'no', we've not established if we're friends or just indifferent, we must watch our heads and feet, maybe the danger's new, insidious. Builds up.

*

We ask a guy, 'Hey, my good friend, friend so we hope – we're interested in where the army's gone, and if there's people taking people off the streets.'

'You guys been away a while?' he asks suspiciously. 'My name is Armand, call it like it's Almond, if it helps.'

We thank him, we don't give our names – Dan said you tell how things are by seeing if there's names on stores and buildings. Armand says,

'There's always demos here. I'll show you, if you want. I think the guys go home when all is done. It's hard to tell – you can't expect to tag them all!'

'That guy's like you,' Fay says to Apple, brusquely. 'The ones that say don't know or can't – is all called fruits or flowers! Almond! It's like when I was a suspect.'

'What of?' asks Apple, fascinated.

'Oh, I don't remember anything,' says Fay, offhand. 'It's the way your brain's wired up – can't do anything about it, what you remember, what you tell.'

'I'm sure ...' says Gus,

'Well, good for you,' says Fay. 'Just don't tell

about Dan's plan. A State for everyone who'd rather be without, but still have certainty, the gossip, someone to look for you when you go lost. Going down south, with cattle too, don't mention it ...'

Mr Silverside says that she's paranoid, but maybe that is right, who can tell what's in our heads, still less what's in the books we read, that gives us brotherhood we haven't earned, maybe.

Dan says it's not the weird ones that get caught, it's those that do the ordinary things – and Armand says,

'There aren't no fighting that I've heard. Nor people being lifted off the streets. There is compassion, just about for all.'

'Well, there you are,' says Mr Silverside. 'We'll sort you out and clean you off and fit you in. No doubt it can be done. Just seek the truth, a guy will tell it you. Truth cuts reality down to size, remember that.'

'Keep pushing?' Fay says. 'That sounds weak.'

'I gave up,' says Apple. 'That took courage too.'

I say to Mr Silverside, 'It seems to me you moralise too much. The thing must be – avoid with dignity the things awaiting you. Encourage others, too. That seems to follow, though there's those, like Gus, who say the path is one you must take singly, cogitating on your own, not generalise.'

Gus nods. He's pondering what to do. We're in a market now, there's boxes here to stack, a job attached to each. He sees, he thinks, employment; and Silverside is pushing him aside, and says, scooping us all in, his thought –

'The trouble is, your undistinguished lives, the periods of pondering, no self-improvement, no deep thoughts at all, and generally the humble exercise of activities quite at, beyond, the limit of the good, the edifying. Find a noble soul, a cause, and follow it. Look, here's the guys that's been demobbed, they did some duty, love of homeland, keep us safe, all that. So, do you think they'll rampage now, up and down and burn the place?'

Apple says it takes more than a fire to burn those buildings down. 'Stand by with dignity,' she starts to say ... and that word, it fires in Armand, and he says, 'Yes! If you don't want to watch the soldiers, there are demos, dignity comes in, I'm sure.'

This Armand seems a guy you wonder if there's soul inside.

'He seems a cool, enlightened guy,' says Apple. 'There's a smell of massacre about him.'

'Come, come,' says Mr Silverside, pushing us along. 'There's nothing new, that in the mass the species is quite cruel, but individuals who think that way are rare; they wear it on their skin,' and Dan objects, 'It's circumstance, is all,' but Mr Silverside just shouts, 'Come on, my squad, we'll settle you to rights, and truth shall be your guide,' and Gus says it isn't guidance that he wants, and, till we're settled, leave the species stuff aside.

'No chivalry, no shame, and no disgrace,' says Dan.

'That's what my travels taught, the future should give that.'

'Those Indians – they don't agree,' says Fay. 'They're each a link – pleasing the spirits, leaving children, getting to the end all in one piece – that is their aim. I hope that when I'm gone, someone will take my memories – I've struggled hard, I wouldn't want to lose them.'

'Well,' says Gus. 'I found the truth – my origins have melted right away, and what's the good of that?' and I say Fay's memories are rubbish, who'd want them, if that was a possibility, and then I ask,

'I called on Mr Silverside – what do we want from him, what are we? What will we become? A moral force? Assassins, actors? – or helpers in a store?'

'Well,' says Apple. 'That's certainly a lot of choice. Those are exciting futures. Fay – will you remember how we thought of each suggestion, or will you wait to see how it turns out?'

Fay says, 'I think I'll go along a certain way with what turns up. And hope extravagant things will happen, but not so brutal that they sweep us all away.'

Armand has drifted off, and Apple says, 'What a bland boy, it makes me long to make him loved, a secret thing, intense and touching, undiscerned by him when he is living it, but maybe letters left, a diary even,' and Gus says that's the oddest thing he's heard.

*

Soon it's clear Armand's gone to the police – and we are crowded in their room.

'We didn't steal a thing,' says Dan. 'Nor steal and throw away. As for beliefs ...'

The problem is, the cop can't speak our language well. Silverside is at the door, he bargains, but we can't hear what he says.

The cop says, 'Tell me what you did, and maybe want to do,' and we don't understand. Dan says we don't deal in generalities, but that's not true. The cop says it's a lie, for everyone does that, it's what we must face up to – and the law is interested in the broadest things, intent and guilt, all that.

'No, no, good man,' says Apple. 'We may get to that in time. First, you must ask specific things.'

'No, no,' says the guy. 'If you're after information, you must fish, and only torture when the yield is slight. You start with a broad picture, if you haven't that, then law and finding out is not your fort.'

'No, no,' says Gus. 'It's not your "fort" like fortress – it's Italian, and it means your strength.'

'No, no,' the cop says. 'My strength you will discover, if it's inner or just brute. It's now you're in my fortress, you're just jelly things, quite average, denying everything.'

'They'll never let us out,' says Fay. 'We don't

know anything, we're innocent – there is no hope.'

*

Hope or not, they let us leave. Mr Silverside is jovial: he says. 'There! I bet you peed yourselves, courageous ones! You're purified, they've nothing on you, but you're known – now, you can do anything.'

Fay says, 'There's so much to concern us – the State, cows, case. The bands of Indians. Armed insurrection ... How fortunate those demented – they can deny and shake their heads with calm,' and Silverside says,

'Well, cops never torture you – that's just a thing,' and he squints at me, 'Invented by the papers. Besides, the Indians, this time it's a farce! It's all been lived through and survived – there's bigger things now to cause anxiety: sun and earth, the galaxy ...'

'Where do wc go?' asks Fay, unconsoled. 'I've had my lover, and my past. What's left?'

Gus says, 'Fay, life is a strip, like a conveyor belt. It's not a mountain, struggled up and then down quick bang on your backside. Dementia's not eternal present, it is present, sure, but it's no-Fayland,' and she is not consoled.

'All I want to know is how to get things,' says Fay.

'Apple even lost her footing,' Dan laughs.

'I wanted to show you guys how to attain,' I say. 'I didn't make it, so it's up to Mr Silverside.'

*

'Goddam!' says Mr Silverside. 'You lot are talented! Destined for the tops. Fay, years on the road and on peyote. Dan, discovering those guys who wanted to stay hidden. Apple, diving from icy heights into a barrel. And you,' he makes to poke me in the eye, 'spying for Albania.'

'It hasn't left its marks,' I say, and Fay is mumbling 'Marx, Marx? Where did our experience go? What did we learn? What did we teach?'

'Onward now,' says Mr Silverside, quite firmly. He goes on,

'See, if I ask, "how many monsters come out of the cave?" – you can't answer, but you understand, and you know you can't answer. Until – "there they come!"' Mr Silverside explains, 'It's the balance between – the tension, the battle – between the chance and the general, the intention and the occurrence, the courage it takes to face down the monsters, or to flee them.'

'Yes, yes,' says Apple, and Fay says that tension and battle are quite different, and Mr Silverside agrees. 'The thing is, even as victims, you must be extreme. At the limit, the definition. Don't fear excess – it's all you have, and it will come, you'll bring it on – it comes all by itself.'

'Extreme! Oh yes!' says Gus. 'Like where we were.'

'Yes, Gus, I left you out,' says Silverside. 'Yes you were traveller, explorer, and what you found was ice, a land, a mass of ice, mass that disappeared a flash after you had found it. "Land, land!" you cried – and Lo! the land was water.'

I say, 'Where will you lead us, Mr Silverside?' and even as I ask, there's Armand running after – to apologise? Unlikely. To extend some questioning that cannot lead to answers, a 'what will you do?', a 'what did you intend?'

He jostles, headlong lad, and Silverside is falling, falling.

He falls into a trench.

'Oh no,' cries Dan, 'I've seen it many times – a trap, banal, a hole – and at the bottom, death.'

It's true, it seems, for Silverside is silent. His face a half-moon, showing bluish white, the other part submerged.

'And should we turn him?' Apple asks.

'No, no,' says Fay. 'That is the perfect pose. It suits him to the ground, and even under.'

'Where shall we go?' wails Apple.

'We should alert the cops,' Armand says, 'but I am halfway one, so maybe that's enough?'

Meanwhile Gus is filleting the pockets of the dead: 'It is our ancient custom,' and he's found an envelope, a parchment, contract – something ...

Silverside's still silent, gives no sign of what he wanted, where we were to go, the lives to live.

'Well, that's the point,' says Fay. 'The end displays the purpose,' but we cannot follow her. We run, and Armand too, and Mr Silverside for sure was monster of his own invention, back in his hole. Like all the monsters, that, he was born to be.

*

'Initial pain, lasting dependence,' that's what Silverside's last testament forewarned.

'No, Fay,' I say. 'Not you, nor anyone of us – don't put those needles in your ears.'

The value Mr Silverside had left was not invention – that made us rich, and deals with waves, and tiny things you nearly cannot see. Reminds us of that saying, 'on your wavelength', which was meant to be agreement, but it really means – cross purposes, white noise. His real treasure – his organigram. An institution, with Divisions – each one of us a General, of course. I'm top. Dan is in packaging, Apple gives displays, Fay makes the contracts, Dan rattles his army – those Indians, if we should need them. Armand we park outside: security, and hope he may be shot.

The profits are quite fabulous. Each of us is rich, but busy too, and so it doesn't count. We sell the secret, some of it, to guys who can't work out what it's all about. Wealth! Like the tide.

It's simple. The apparatus – needles for your ears, and wires – it lets you read your thoughts. No, not someone else's, not communication – that has all been done before. It's narcissus: in the raw, excited, analytical. That's what everybody wants – to understand themselves, the things that creep out of their brain, then creep back in again.

'Some guys are worshipping dear Mr Silverside,' says Apple.

'That is what he'd want,' I say. 'It's right. They're right.' We think of that bright dying face, the other half obscured and in the mud. The trilby, slowly sinking, never to be worn again. 'The pathos!' Apple says.

We have a ceremony – is it a month, already? All that cash, lodged here and there, in bales, in sacks where we can help ourselves, if only there were things we want ...

'This is sad,' says Fay. 'I cannot stand the sense of being here enclosed, success, the long "so what".'

I make the speech – I say, 'My friends, I love you all ...' and Apple asks. 'Does that mean we should love you?' I say,

'It's true I'm icon, but you must remember – it's Silverside, our inspiration, giving life that we might prosper,' and there's applause, yes! my genius, my modesty ... I am a cult! Gus says,

'I use the money well, it buys me cows,' and soon our needles and the cord are universal, our partners buy and buy – into our secrets, not grasping much, the how and why, but money clinks or shuffles in – and maybe reading your own thoughts can serve, it's not like reading other guys', or sending letters fast, whatever that may do.

'It's surely democratic, everyone is wanting one,' I say, not caring much. But we've no time to read our thoughts. We – only we, the Generals – we have no doubts, and every twist and hitch of ganglia is known, familiar.

For me, the scheme will cease when we are rich, or poor, and Fay sobs in her office, 'Oh how sad, this death, this sitting here and idiots coming in and out, and maybe I'm an idiot too,' and Gus and Apple park and stack their cows and plan to leave, and Dan says that his Indians are getting bored, their thoughts opaque or forked and furious ... Thoughts are all the same to them. They don't join in our scheme. Thoughts come, they go. The Indians don't worship Mr Silverside.

*

Fame, riches.

Fay says we were better with the case, you pick it up and run, your wealth comes too.

I say to Dan,

'This thought stuff – certainly, that Silverside had something on the truth – he pointed out the way, the path. But in the end ... They must have filled him in ... that trench – his silver side, his half-moon face, eclipsed for good. Yes, his trilby and his cane no more – ah yes, the pathos! Apple's right. All's done and ended.

'It seems to me you're right – that State, those warriors, Dan,' I say. 'They're quite a thing that's more grown up,' and he agrees. 'Let's think of leaving this,' I say, and wave my hands. The sacks of cash, Armand out there, awaiting bandits, all a-tremble ...

*

Our users seem to want a discipline – that ancient tale of unity, the time and place, the moral purpose, character – how they love all that! Enough of them!

I say, 'Time to move on, Apple and Gus, we'll ride your cows down South, like true cowboys. We'll sing and let our thoughts run wild and free, over the plains, into the sky, and Mr Silverside ...'

'Is dead,' cries Apple, and she's moved. Dan says,

'Those photos that we took of us – they'll do fine now, a tribute to the master and his paper trail, all hail! to Silverside,' and so we spread those photos everywhere, the three of us that was, and somewhere there, the suitcase ...

'Yes, yes,' I say. 'Let's close it off, this panoply, the lackeys that we've hired, the gold and diamonds on the walls: enough! Armand forever at the door, expecting destiny. We'll take those sacks of cash ...'

Fay says, 'Sacks, sacks? You mean the tax! We haven't paid,' and Gus says now's the time to move, we should've thought – Dan's state doesn't cost a cent, you just plug in or not.

'Yes, this is the time to disappear,' says Apple. 'Now, we have left a hint, a revelation, an epiphany – you straighten out your thought, and then reflect again, where does that lead, what good ...?' and on she goes, it's time to leave indeed, for Apple's founding sects and raising doubts. Perhaps some guys will come and take those sacks and make us work some more,

'You idiots,' shouts Gus. 'You've left your mugshots everywhere, those photos ... Quick, put on these cowboy hats, bandanas on your face, and off we'll go ...'

'The case, the case ...' wails Fay, 'is closed,' says Apple, firm.

*

We walk down South – a land secure, says Gus, jumping up and down on it – no water here, no ice, no treachery. The South – a land of song – and chance.

Here, there are Indians – Dan says that he could found a state, no difficulty, the Indians here are into gaming, and I say, 'You'd better not insist – be very prudent, Dan.'

Fay says, 'Oh no, those cows, poor creatures, what a fate. It's true they're food, but we're their executioners.'

'Fay, you're quite a sentimental soul,' I say.

'Alas, my Dan is out of reach,' she says. 'I'll maybe cosy up to you, like all that time ago.' I think, that that's a losing bet, aside from cows we've nothing left, the platinum, the case – it languishes in airport or in depot ... Emotions deposited as well.

Fay insists, 'I'm so content with you, I've seen you boss the guys around when you were rich – such character, your thoughts as straight as arrows in the sky.'

There's Indians, they organise the gaming right and left, they run a diner too. 'Throw of the Dice', and Apple says that she and Gus could maybe wait on tables here, and sell the cows, quite slowly, one by one, and Fay says that's all right, a compromise, the beasts will scarcely notice, and their fate's by lot, better than that you cannot have.

We say farewell, and Apple says she'll exercise no more, her body's left, parked in the kitchen, unadventurous. She cries, and we would cry with her. We don't.

The gas station here's right at the edge of town, it's called 'Last Chance'. We're independent of it, and the three of us, Fay, Dan and I, we camp. A river trickles by. The cows are gone, we cuddle up, the evening's cool, the moon climbs up – we think of Mr Silverside. He didn't help us find the case, but set us on our way.

Fay's quite a beauty here, the 'being quite unique' must suit. The moon is small and mean, a dime, and not a dollar in the sky.

'Oh, it will grow,' says Fay. 'You must insist, you'll always find a guy who takes you in, and keeps you warm.'

*

In the distance, the sun lights up the cones, cubes, pyramids, of Memphis town. There is no song. Fay says,

'Some dreams – they have been lost. Poor Apple – her gymnastics, they are at an end.'

'Well', I say. 'It's true Dan's in a silent patch, it's maybe for the best. But he'll come bursting in again ... His painless State will rise, he'll find some warriors ... At least, we're all alive, they could have killed us all. They often do.'

'That's paranoid,' Fay says, and brightens up. 'Not even Armand met the destiny that he deserves.'

And then – we think of Mr Silverside. 'Yes, he went down,' says Fay. 'There was our fortune, there it went. He's somewhere up there, I am sure, outspreads the means to straighten out our thoughts ...'

We meditate on straightened thoughts.

'We have each other, starting off again,' Fay says. 'Remember the demented – "After the ball ..."' She laughs.

'If I were you, dear loving Fay,' I say, 'I wouldn't bet on me. You'll maybe lose.'

*

Later, together we watch the screen, Fay and I. Desolation.

The baritone hits, maybe he forms, some membrane, some thicker air. It divides his nothing from ours. Does it come, pulsing, from him? Is it a barrier, filter, there already? The voice, a wave, nothing into nothing. How far from us he is ... yet there's a structure in between us, made by him, or maybe springing up by nature. A nothing quite insubstantial, transparent scaffolding that falls into a silence, a void. What has it been, what could it be, the voice forever dropping nothing into nothing? Ears, brain, mind, – nets to catch what quickly falls and passes by. Off the singer's page. Into space – maybe buzzing with the particles, unseeable, they say are swarmed around us.

Another picture ... the court ... a loose fouetté here and there. Reassuring that the dancers are all Russians, very tall. Limbs like pine branches. Concentration – though the music seems quite fidgety. The magic spell they confab over – I know it can be broken, quite easily. Maybe they know it too. They're up in lifts, not the electric kind, don't want to come down from them, but they must.

The screen says it's *Jeudi*: game day.

Here, scenes of people speaking a kind of French. Black earnest pitted faces, white American ones smoothing it out, speakeasily, taking misfortune on the mouth.

Games – the plants, their tendrils worming into babies' beds, their berries covered with saliva, sperm: masked, hooded. They're playing, or they think they play, those flowers. It's game day. Tomorrow the friar comes, black and dry from the woodcut. Cut by woodcutters – who else? Such skills, lost. We'd so much hope – now, we can't picture things unless they're lost.

In every story there's a 'responsible', someone like Mr Silverside, rarely do you get the better of them ... or the worse. They have the power.

'Not everything's a story,' says Mr Silverside's

ghost.

I say, 'You don't need women with the sight to tell you when your time is up. Maybe you moderns, living in time eternal – maybe you have no shape.'

Silverside goes on, 'You're always part of someone's five, know it or not. Friends – one, more creative than you, waiting for their tragic end. A failed lover – you bounce off them like an empty bottle tossed against a wall. One – is your conscience. One – a wild card. And one, a friend you want and can't express to ...'

*

I wake up, not very drunk.

*

'Endings!' says Fay. 'If you start something, it has to have an ending, or you have to give it one. Music always has one, paintings never do – they're all ending anyway. Books end,' she says wisely, and I say,

'Careful, Fay, the ending may be you. What you mean is climax, some dénouement, a sense you've gone from light to dark, or black to gloss. In short ...' I say, irritated. 'You're supposed to know more at the end than at the start, not just things in between, stuff gets folded in, left ready to consume, just like a pancake. The ending's not a "flop", into a hole ...'

'I guess it's education, then,' she says. 'That doesn't make you better, just informed, like what is two by two.'

'It's as you wish, young Fay,' I say.

*

'Soon it'll be our birthdays,' I say. 'And we'll see Apple.'

'That doesn't follow,' Fay says. 'However, much you may prefer her. And that experience you had with her – what does it matter now, if had or imagined?'

'It ought to matter,' I say. 'Though I don't know who'd care. It's like the truth – maybe Mr Silverside had some, about some thing – though it certainly wasn't in his pockets ...' and we meditate on cash and fame, both lost through oversight or maybe wishing so. 'Telling the truth,' I say. 'It seems to call out some commitment, though if you know it, don't tell it, or just lie – I'm not so sure there is a punishment attached.'

'Quiet!' says Fay. 'Who knows if it's out there, truth, or in your telling it.'

*

We turn back to the screen: 'The rivers, the wells, Fay,' I say. 'Poisoned or dry. Look! There's nothing showing but the movies about nomads, leaving their hot dry mountains. Their sick animals. Small wars coming.'

'I'd go up there,' she says. 'Not to be simple, but to be free.'

'That's what they used to say,' I say. 'It takes lots of special knowledge to be destitute.'

'No, no,' she says. 'I'd make do. I'd buy their clothes and sell them in the valley, on a stall.'

'You need a faith,' I say. 'Another thing you haven't got.'

She presses on. 'That Buddha now, I feel he had an angle. Not like Jesus, getting pinned up on his first big gig ...'

'It's not you're wholly ignorant,' I say. 'It's just you know wrong stuff.'

*

Gus and Apple step in, gesturing, their eyes black-rimmed, as if they just peeled off from silent movies.

Behind them there's a guy – is that a leopard-spotted frock coat that he wears, doing some business with his hands?

'Hurrah for retro,' Fay exclaims, and Gus says,

'We threw up our crap jobs, to drop in on our birthday party,' and they've brought a cake. 'Happy for ever, Elvis,' on the top. Apple says,

'It's true we stole it, but he never comes. He'll reign for ever, king of kings. Those awful songs. They put the cakes down by his pyramid in Memphis, but who cares?'

Gus points, and says, 'This weird guy here is Frederson. A relative of Freder – you remember him? The movie star! Metropolis! He's dropped by too, to show us stuff.'

'We did all that,' says Fay. 'And did for Mr Silverside. Still, I want to be everything, be shown – a worker, boss, an artisan. I've tried most things, another one would suit me well.'

I say, 'The things you've done, Fay – nothing sticks,' and Frederson unfolds his voice, it comes from circuses and brawls, and says,

'The rushing water doesn't stick, my friend, it washes dirty and it washes clean. It's as indifferent as Fay – collecting stuff to sell it on.' The mighty sound he makes – it overwhelms, it chases bats from caves beneath the sea. I say,

'Fay doesn't sell, she just consumes.'

Frederson makes the finger sign that shows he is

about to speak of Elvis.

'That poor guy,' he says. 'He sang and sang. He couldn't manage other things.'

'Like what?' asks Fay.

'Well,' says Frederson, expanding. 'There's climbing peaks and skiing down. Or sitting by the sea, to count the waves. Those things will take your bucks and send you back refreshed to make some more. The actual ruling isn't done on beach or mountain,' he explains. 'That's where the losers go, to fly on kites or in balloons, or little pencil cases in the sky. The kings! – ah yes, you follow those, and help design the pyramid where you will rest eternally, your good work done.' He contemplates, he smiles. A day's work done, and well, he thinks. Those kings ...

'The trouble with you Europeans, or would-be so,' he carries on. 'Is – it's all done!'

'We're not from Europe, not especially,' I say. 'Gus here – he doesn't even have a continent. If Coldland's where he's from, it's all just slush and carcasses.'

Frederson presses ahead: 'Wherever you guys came from, that is where you got your gods, your rhetoric, your sitting up to watch the silent movies ... from when the world was young and gestural. That's why I'm retro, showing when it was it started running down. The killing and the sex ... those wars, the hair ...'

He speaks for hours – the empires dwindling, lashing out, religious wars, the currencies decline and fall, dashed down ...

'Yes, yes,' says Fay. 'We know all that. Enough! Remake our innocence, or else be quiet.'

'Your trouble is, dear Fay,' says Frederson, who's quite at home and eats our cake. 'That first you wanted truth, now – innocence. First – to do nothing: truth is not a thing to hang on walls. There is no clock to punch with truth. But innocence – well, you do everything to lose it, quick as quick. It's quite the contrary of truth.'

'That too you cannot hang on walls,' says Apple.

Frederson swings round on her. 'Oh yes, my sweet – those masks, the paintings with the primal scrawls, the kiddies' pictures – solid house. just one door – the sun, the storm, the moon, all overhead. There, that's where your innocence went.'

'Silverside – he made us rich,' says Apple. 'Were we loved as well? I'm not so sure.'

'Rich? That wasn't anything,' says Frederson. 'A gadget you invented, by stealing it from Silverside. No, if you're loved, you have to wait and see. When you are dead.'

'That seems a flaw,' says Gus. 'I'm not sure being rich or loved is what I want,' and Frederson roars out,

'That too, you'll have to wait and see.'

*

'Apple falls lots more now,' says Gus, 'It makes her still more interesting. Into the crackers and the soup.'

*

Dan comes thrusting in. His fears are all around him. 'Hi, you idle hopefuls,' he says, unconvinced, 'Now the jungle's stripped away, I still don't feel master of myself. Those new huts! Those machines, all yellow in the yellow. Dust to mud and mud to dust. But – don't lose heart, there's more and more – guys who'd like to get away.'

'And they're not following, not you nor anyone at all,' says Frederson, who seems to know everything.

Dan says, 'When I'm hunted, I am not so brave – but now, it's roads and rules and offices – I'm terrified.'

'That's not at all the scene, that I had heard,' says Fay, rounding on him. 'If you want warmth, then go and start a fire.'

I tell Apple, 'I'm so full of things to say, I can't say any of them.' I mean to say, maybe she's winding down, the falling, some memories dropping out ... But still, there is the two of us, our story? And she says,

'At last! You've lost, I hated you as boss, and now you're quite cut down to size, and reasonable. I'm fortunate – that Gus mends all I break. But he's so passive – those solids, melted into water, there's nothing left, no new, no old.'

I think – it's scarcely overtures she's giving me, but I go on, and there's a shout, it's Apple, and she screams,

'You hugged me!' and I say, quite softly, 'That was all part of the plan.'

The consequence is terrible, the others stare, and Frederson rears up, a yellow spotted emperor, and says,

'Well, well, it's time for music chairs, I see. We all change partners – it's my turn with Fay.' I say,

'It's quite perverse, but – take her – with that voice you'll shout her down!' and maybe Frederson is carrying some balm, restorer of her years, you palm it on, her crags and valleys all dissolve, she's almost innocent again, and she is fetching, like she was when first she worked the bars.

Then Apple says to me, 'Now! Know your place. It isn't next to me. Remember how you lost our cash, those shares ...'

I say, 'Shares? Shares? You mean those guys who wanted in? On us? You're crazy, Apple, there was no blame, no loss: a tale that took a different twist, is all. Besides, young Fay here – there's her dowry lost and waiting somewhere still, – her case,' and Frederson's alert, he says his secret starts with banning fantasy. Making an image, well, that might seem an affront to some creator gods who're picayune, though it might also seem a flattery. The thought is big, the execution always marred. But fantasy is worse – imagining that things might be, or could have been, alternative to plans divine. A turning upside down, big change – all that. It is a real no-go.

And so, it seems we're back to truth and what is real. Fay's case is the object of desire for Frederson, so, is it real, or somewhere lost, unfindable? And yet those armies buried in the sand, the wrecks beneath the sea, that stuff is all dredged up. And so – a case, is that so hard to find?

'What if you don't believe the plan's divine?' I ask.

'What you believe is of no consequence,' says Frederson, quite firm: 'It falls into the category of fantasy, your belief. Or believing you have no belief...'

'I see,' says Dan to Frederson. 'You are a rigorous soul, and we shall suffer mightily from what you teach. It's useful, though, and maybe helps to overcome our fear.'

Then Fay asks Gus, 'Where'd you attract this guy?' and Gus is silent. Apple says, 'He's crazy for the pecan pies, down there in Memphis town. He didn't pay, but offered us that he would prophesy and do some wondrous things,' she says she'd gladly pay two bucks, is what he owed, but he has followed them, it seems his search for fortune isn't fantasy at all, but sought objectively.

Apple says, 'I'm tired of all this country stuff, modernity as well, and "wait and see what history brings", and plans and Frederson, his clothes, his acting like a boss and victim both,' she does some exercises on the floor, and twists her lovely limbs this way and that – directions never seen, a pain to watch, but issuing from a reservoir of tricks and skills unique to her, my dearest Apple, trembling on the bough or rolled up tight, and wheeling down the hills, the arms and legs tucked in all neat ... forget those silly things that balance out our wobbly cores, the limbs ...

I wonder if she's serviced Frederson, upon the mat. While Gus pretends to sleep.

*

'I have no fantasy,' says Apple.'But being double-jointed, maybe I don't need ... Gus has no imagination – I guess that puts him tops for lack of fantasy? I guess the truth is too ambitious – everyone has had their say on that. I think we should have kept more of that money, though.'

Gus says, 'It's true that Frederson appears a chancer – but that does not exclude that he'll take us some place good. His technique – wow, starting with the pie, it took our Apple in. So, now we're here, all three, and unemployed again.'

*

'You guys are pretty unamerican,' Frederson starts off, 'Now – America, in one of the original feathery tongues means "Everywhere", or maybe "Here we are". That's pretty clear. This continent, it gave you self. Your selves. You're stuck with that,' and there's a clamour,

'Gift? Is it a gift? I remember being born, it was an intimate affair, no rhetoric involved.' 'No, no, I sprang up alien and foreign – I wanted none of neighbours, places – those dull main streets ...'

'I came by sea.'

'I walked.'

We hear Dan say, 'I tried the jungle, and I lost. It lost.'

'Look, Frederson,' says Apple. 'While you're waiting to lead, to cheat us of our cash or maybe just to pass the time – you haven't understood. I'll make it easy for you. What is time? A dimension – if we didn't have it, we would fall out of ourselves, we wouldn't last or be. Then – we come along, we human guys: there's history time. Now, time is on the clock, it makes us go to work, and do the things we do, but mostly work. That clock is complex – inside there's wheels and such. But – a clock's a clock, it's everywhere, it's our dimension. Now, Frederson, you understand?'

'No, not at all,' he says.

'It's just a metaphor,' I say, helping him along.

'No, no,' says Fay, 'I've got it – it is Capital, it's what we're in, it is the wiring in our heads.'

'No, no,' says Dan, 'It's not inside, it's over us, it is our end and our beginning.'

'Well,' says Frederson, 'It seems you can't agree. At any rate, it's there, you're here. Or should I say, it's here, you're here. So, what's the deal? We'll always have those clocks, dear Apple. Ever more accurate.'

Apple is cast down. I say, 'It's not a metaphor, it's a kind of analogy.'

Fay says, 'It's clear and obvious – you just remember how the argument goes,' and Frederson says, 'Hmmm, Fay. something inside you vacillates, though when it comes to housing, you've an iron will.'

'Frederson,' says Dan, 'it's up to you. Show us your meaning,' and Frederson mumbles, that his look is like Micawber's, and Gus tells him no, it's the actor that portrayed him long ago, and there's the fantasy, call it hope, despair, conviction – it is all around.

'Let's not hear about starting a commune,' says Fay. 'Farming, baking, painting pots. The squabbling. Do we plant red radishes or white.'

Dan says, 'The Indians as guardians of the state? A fine idea, but blown to air. My mind turns to philosophers – call them kings without a kingdom ...' and Fay shouts out,

'Dan, don't you see? It's all a simulacrum. You brilliant guy – it's all the same idea in different clothes – over again, and over. Your fear? It always turns out bad. Too little nobility, too little innocence? Too much? That's you. Either we drone along and nothing much – or else the guys will up their 'planes, and down we'll go.'

Dan asks, 'When were those noble times? And were they innocent? To me, it is not so.'

Frederson's impatient. 'Come along,' he says, and down we go.

We see some guys, they're idling round on sacks, and smoking cobs and meerschaums, there's gals with golden combs and actor's boots – they're strutting round – and in a pit, there's big machines, they turn and grunt like hippos in a slough.

'You see,' says Frederson. 'Machines do all the work – those guys and gals get paid for lounging there. So, where's your beef?' and at that word, Apple reacts: 'It's true, it's true. We treated them just like machines, those cows. We ate them, but they live on long, they're in our consciences, encysted ...'

'No, no,' says Gus, 'That's just a trick, old Frederson: in those machines there are the spirits of the dead,' and Fay says all that pay must come from somewhere, if it's going spare, she'll have it too.

'No, no,' says Apple. 'Things don't just stop with those machines and paying guys who watch – it grows and grows, machines don't procreate, they're swapped, changed, like the cows, when they run down,' and Frederson is chastened, and he says,

'Well, here's a scene without a fantasy ... of course, there's lots of stuff I haven't shown,' and Fay declares, 'We must get out. We can't. We run, we compromise. And still the urge ... to leave, to try out something different. The planes, machines that bundle us in killer vans, in camps,' and Dan puts in, 'The jungle too,' and Fay says hush! that's just anxiety displaced, the guys that want those trees, they'll sort the jungle out.

Gus concedes, 'It's just like Frederson says – there is no torture here, no guys that bully you. Unease comes from within, from each of us.'

I say, 'It wasn't Frederson, it was Silverside said that, or maybe Almond. Armand.'

Apple says, 'Well, I forget these things,' and Fay says, 'I wish I could. Forget.'

'Movies, and all that singing. It makes you think,' says Dan, 'It's not all innocent.'

'Well,' I say, 'I'm sure all will soon drift away. We're not really here and in one place, we think of all the other places, some of them we wish we're in, and others not at all. I've never really known – what is a country, how you're supposed to feel about them.'

Frederson sums up, 'You have to live in one, keep quiet about it, even if you've friends.'

*

Frederson holds forth, majestic in the coat, Micawber's gown, that smells of movies long reeled up, he walks upon the rim – some cup, a mixing bowl, that churns.

He falls! He's folded in, like jam inside a pancake.

'Oh no!' we cry. And what's inside is stuff for dental moulds – we see it pinky-white and dense.

'My! What a useless thing!' says Gus. 'We turn off the machine, the stuff goes hard as porphyry, and Frederson is set for life, for death, that voice magnificent is whirling upwards to the stars.'

The paddles give a loud whap! whap! 'No no,' some guy exclaims. 'Don't turn it off, he'll set to stone,' but it's too late, Apple has pressed the switch.

'You shouldn'ta done that,' says the guy. 'Useless it is, but what it's for – you ask the boss,' and Apple says at least it shows how Micawber's always right, something unexpected does turn up. The guy butts in again, and says here's private property, that's why they smoke, and Fay says,

'There's a lesson for us all – that pecan pie can spoil your teeth, and more,' and Dan says destiny is sure, it comes, sooner or later, in grotesque moments and designs.

A last 'whap whap,' no sound or sight of Frederson, he's all mixed in. Gus says,

'That's where old movies get you, first there's fantasy – how I remember him, that actor guy! – and then there's silence set in porphyry. And not a song to cheer us on our way.'

‘Another accident,’ says Gus. ‘Frederson – dressed up as another, and himself a fiction. No need to report – if we all ’fessed up to accidents, guys like Armand would never have their peace. Nor give us ours.’

‘Besides,’ says Apple, ‘Frederson would never have ended up as a poetic destiny, in mouths and sung. That machine’s no use, it’s only standing there, it churns and waits for accident.’

Dan says his message anyway was crap – most everything is fantasy once it’s gone inside your head, and living free – well, that’s a puzzle that he’s working on.

*

Later, Fay says, reading out, ‘“In poor nations, the people are comfortable, in rich nations they are generally poor.” That stuff about the working stiffs, that they do well in countries that is poor, there’s crap, for starts. The thing is clear, you put your money into folks – they die, just like machines. The system’s this – make sure the stuff accumulates, not in machines or guys or stuff, it has to be eternal, or it doesn’t count. And if you buy some slaves, or pick some fruit – the fun you get, it lasts a year at most ...’

‘Yes, yes,’ I say, not kindly. ‘Fay, we know all that. Tell us how we, who are not chic, nor part of some exotic crowd, may start from zero,' and she laughs, and says, 'Well, zero's like that guy who saw the beauties in the road, the case we lost, the photos that we took: it doesn't add, or calculate.'

I'm sure there's lots like us. 'Radical guys!' says Dan. 'It seems it's Saint Augustine, maybe Doctor Caligari – they said it all before. The end must come, and while it comes, it crushes ... the new Indians, they don't want me ...'

'Well, Dan, that is another point, and as it should be too,' says Gus.

'There's no way out, it has to end first,' Apple says. 'And I'll not be around.'

*

Mr Silverside – he had the secret of the cash – but then he died. Frederson – he knew the system can survive if fantasy, desire is blocked. But then the system's blocked as well. Desire that's stopped is gratified – so, there's the loop, desire sets you rushing to the end. Fay says, 'And love has passed. And Apple skates. And Gus's land has disappeared. It's left to you.' She points at me. I point at Dan.

'This heavy useless talk,' says Apple, 'My time is up. The train – though I'm not going anywhere ...'

I turn to Dan, ignoring her – 'The trouble is, with all your schemes, directed at some unknown guys, emarginated, volatile – all turn upon the state, and as you know, it's not the state that signifies, it is its Geist, its spirit ...'

'Or its ghost,' says Dan. 'That's me.'

The train – 'It doesn't stop here ...'

Apple's warned: she says, 'Well no, but it must pass.'

*

We talk and talk of Dan's new plan, and then a guy comes in to say that Apple's dead.

Those loops and downstrokes on her skateboard, so careful and so concentrated. Then the train ...

'Oh no!' says Gus. 'Not under, all chopped up ...'
'She went into the side, she's fresh,' the guy says. 'Accident, for sure.'

Gus says, 'She shouldn't have – a sacrifice, it wasn't her that pushed those guys, not Mr S, not Frederson, the ghost from movies past – she couldn't wait another interval, another act ...'

Dan says that Gus should know if guys are pushed, he's always up behind them, arms outstretched. I say,

'Dan's state that lacked a Geist – well, now it has one. Apple's spirit, fresh, released,' and Fay asks if the ghosts know if they are alive or dead, and Gus says no, they've no idea, it's us the puzzled ones – we know they're dead, but ghosts act as though they live. That's the thing with abstracts, it appears – you never know their state of health. And then we realise that Apple's dead, that she will talk to us, but talking to her's useless, dead is dead ...

'Alas,' says Dan. 'She couldn't choose between us – so she chose the train.'

'Nonsense,' says Gus. 'She was an artist. She died as she should, seeking perfection, or at least more speed.' I add, 'She made us feel our bodies quite intensely – even as we were feeling hers. Youth! Away the years, all the wrinkles, the steaming pits – a frolic, like the seals, or cod ...'

There's a shocked silence, as they say.

Dan and Gus ask 'Bodies? Where did those come in?'

Dear Apple.

*

We have to go to Armand. It seems he is a cop – maybe he always was.

He asks, 'Yes. What is accident? The unexpected? Is it only that, what you guys had not foreseen? Something unnatural? Or all too natural, like falling down a hole. Apple now – she went up like a match. Friction, you see. Is that the cause? And is it friction that we blame? Or skateboards? Maybe it is best to blame poor Apple. What is 'push'? Those guys from silent movies, promising you fortunes – or some gravity?' On he goes. He's been promoted, so he's dressing down. Cheap shoes.

I see upon his desk a ruffled manuscript: 'Report on the revolutionary movement of the toiling masses of the East.'

'You find it interesting?' Armand asks. I nudge Dan so's to take attention from myself.

'You would say so,' says Armand, going on and on. 'Apple – against the train, like match on scratch ...' A flaming angel.

*

I go to see my Master. Here I am, the posters say 'Sicilia'. He's another, quite like Fay or Dan, who knows everything – though with him, it comes out different.

We hug and pat each other. ‘Why, you’re armed!’ I say, alarmed. His beard is white and warm, you go inside, it’s like a cloud, dry as the tropics.

I remember how they say he was a great *tombeur de femmes*, the *femmes tombées* translated into fallen women. Here’s his house, blue, on the beach, it leans this way and that according to the breeze. He lives alone, unless they share a toothbrush.

‘I’ve come about the premonition, Master,’ and he says we forget extreme gestures, Apple’s, and I ask,

‘Is that what it was? She seemed contained within her body, that single wall – and why could she not speak, and tell the message?’ and he says,

‘That’s where you don’t observe. You – you’re all playing being characters from some old movies, some silent, some now turning black.’

I tell him, ‘Toilers of the East’. He says,

‘They’d better hurry, while there is an East. And while there’s toil.’

‘Armand was my pupil,’ he goes on. ‘Ungainly and ungaining, my only one, the only one I can recall, who calls on me,’ he says. ‘I know you’ve a conspiracy going on. He tells me that,’ and I say,

‘Master, even conspiracy’s worth a try, just tell us what to plot.’

We pause. We sit across from one another. We read each other sections from *The Magic Mountain*. He insists.

'This sets my mind at rest,' he says. 'It's all in there,' he reads it loud and slow. I gabble when it is my turn: we did it all at school. I say,

'It's written well. You have to wait a long time for the jokes. I bet he wrote it without anyone to check the spelling,' and there's more reading, and we go to bed.

Next day, he says, 'No luggage? Very wise. Remember too, never admit to being out of touch. The message? Apple's? Well, she was an inarticulate soul, maybe there was the urge, the apprehension, but no words.'

Hung on the walls, his poems, plasticated, like anatomic specimens, those slices of smoked thigh. I lay a hand on one, it leaves some grease.

Fay said, 'Apple – Oh, how I envy her. The flame, the gesture. Yet – no! I don't, of course.'

Dan said, 'The people? And the State? What those guys want is clear – order and cash. Then if you like, some intricate ideas, but not too many or too complicated.'

I tell the Master all about straight thought, the riches that it brought and lost, how we proposed not equality but equal treatment, and he screws his eyes and fights himself to understand.

'It seems to me there's no sense there,' he says.

We go outside, and on the quay, there's guys that's selling cases, some are empty, most are full of someone's stuff. Fay's isn't there.

'Look, look!' the Master shouts. 'Here comes your boat. It's true that reading *Magic Mountain*, all that stuff – it's rather precious, but we're the last to give it time – the young, alas, their eyes are empty and they suffer silently. I have an orchard round the back, of bergamots – the young guys shoot at me at harvest time, that's why I carry iron ...'

I hop aboard the boat, farewell, farewell, all that. He shouts, 'Get out! Get out, away! And leave! You're not safe here,' but I have left. I understand the message, clear as though it's written down, the spelling checked. Get out.

*

Apple's ghost says, 'All that fuss. Of course, there was some intent – after all, I was there. The tracks. I went there. Some chance too, and not having what you guys have, the seeming to know ... Listen,' Apple's ghost goes on, 'I don't need to talk about that now, I really don't. You can, if you wish, but on your own. It doesn't concern me. Yes, I regret the cows – Gus is so used to killing things.'

*

Fay says, 'Stop turning those stones. No ghosts. No animals reared to die and finish bad, lots thrown in the bin. Think "tigers", not antelopes.'

I say, 'In other times, it would have been quite fun – reading aloud, sleeping on the floor. Like being very young, but this time quite enjoying it. The Master, the books he knows, that don't matter.'

Fay says, 'You go, you come back. Never a little gift for me.'

I say, 'The Master – I guess that's foolish – master of nothing, worried for his bergamots.'

'You have to try,' says Fay, 'Anything. Ghosts and all.'

*

'I'm a dental nurse,' she says, 'In fact, your dental nurse.'

'I got the little traitors fixed,' I say.

'What?' she says.

'Teeth,' I say. I'd waited for her. Waited – to see what would happen. There's little fantasy in it.

She says, 'Of course I like you. This is it. You do what you have to do.'

I say, 'Well, it's done, it seems.'

She says, 'You can't have more than more. It's not all always straight and simple. This time it is.'

*

That was adventure too – my dental nurse. Holding my head while I spat out.

*

Dan says, 'My family sold up. They wanted to be liquid – so I've lots of cash.'

'What's to do?' asks Fay – 'You buying tents for indigenes, or bullets and a flag?'

'I'm not a limpet, Fay, I'm not like you. I'd rather be a shark.'

'Rather! Oh, rawther yes! And how!' she mocks. He says,

'Saving people, shooting people – it's all reckoned to be honourable. Only humiliating people – that's not supposed to happen, but it does, in street and bedroom: it's all practice! It's irrelevant too, shoot, save, save and shoot. It's nature, it's necessity, it's an aesthetic ramp and rumble, it's the flag we carry as we crawl along, dodging the missiles ...'

'It's all people,' Gus interrupts, and Dan says,

'No, no! They live they die, they all die, what they leave is never part of them, it's stuff, ingots or goats, the ownership – it doesn't last, it doesn't count. No, all that matters is the cause – not the goddam people, live or die – it's the faith, the revolution, it's equality, the hierarchy – without that, there's nothing, there's a squirm of blood-filled tubing in the dust, it's mouths and arses, buy and sell, scribble, cancel – screw and flop ...'

'If it's history you're on about,' says Fay, 'you'd better help the Master with his bergamots, and shoot those lazy punks ...'

'No, no,' shouts Dan. 'Not history – that's dead, now it's little twitchy guys with gold and silver stars they're giving out. The point is – battle now: you're present on the scene, and that is reason, wall to wall, and good enough.'

'Well,' says Fay. 'Go to, Dan! Find your stage, and act.'

'My Indians,' says Dan. 'It was a losing cause. The governors, they caught the women when they could, and sterilised them. Guys who didn't end in cages – they'd die childless anyway. So, any scheme fell down.'

Somewhere Apple's ghost says, 'My body was my special care – and I could do no more. So many questions! And I couldn't answer any of them ...'

*

Fay says, 'I want to know what kind of ship I'm on, even if it's sinking.' She reads those cartoon story books. 'Lots of these is worth one *Magic Mountain* – but they're better – like ballet's music and dancing, opera's singing and acting. These are tales and pictures – keeps you busy, following.'

'I know all about ships,' I say, 'after that trip to there and back. The Master and his hot dry beard. Ships – they go voyaging – it's more we're in a castle, under siege. We're safe but hungry till it falls.'

'You think it gives protection?' Dan asks. 'It may be safer outside. Do a deal.'

'Yes,' says Fay. 'I might want to leave. Even have a door open for the guys outside. Maybe they don't want to enter – just circle round, and everything as it was. Skeletons on the ramparts, horizons lost.'

'Apple thought the magic stuff – wisdom, truth, invention – came through the body, not the mind,' I say. 'She would have taken chances, sallied forth.'

'She didn't resurrect,' says Gus. 'Just up in flame, no lesson there, and everything remaining as it was.'

'Are you sure it's a castle we're imagining?' asks Dan. 'It seems only we're in some natural feature without walls.'

'Just look at all the people,' I say, trying to lead him on. 'With their bundles, billhoooks, kids clinging on, waiting to settle, to emigrate, to reach asylum ... Sure, we're in a castle,' and Fay says,

'Look at them, the millions – if you feed them, they acquire a character ...'

'No,' says Dan, playing along. 'They're already domesticated.'

We fall silent.

Fay stares at me. She says, 'I love talking about the Master, the cunning things he said. All long ago, of course. I never met him – but the stuff about the East, China – the great change ...'

'Yes, well, you never met him, Fay,' I say. 'The changes happen, happened, for that you don't need genius.'

'Maybe you just need teeth,' says Fay.

'How'd you know about my nurse?' I ask, amazed.

'I have teeth too, you know,' she says. 'A bad idea of yours, before you even had it.'

'Poor Apple,' Gus says, trying to recall her. 'She was in customer service – that she did, a job like any other. I taught her the song, that became her dream. The great composer of the northland – "when the cows come rolling home ..." Those were the words, became her mantra. Down to Memphis, singing. The symphony – he tried others, but that was the first.'

'People make fun of music,' Fay says. 'But it's something that can't decompose.'

Gus never laughs.

I say, 'Gus! I thought those were Elvis songs we sang, and now it seems it was some Finn, watching his cows.'

He says, 'Apple didn't know the answers – and if I did, who would come to me and ask enlightenment?'

Fay gestures at the TV. 'Those guys on there behind the screen – they want us to support the ones that's shouting "freedom". We bombed their fathers when they did the same – so what? What's changed?'

I say, 'It's all about accumulation, not the good guys here or there – the wealth that swells and moves about, that's what we're following,' and Fay says, 'Well, thanks to you, our hook slipped off our riches,' and I remind her that she lost the suitcase, and we quarrel till Dan says,

'I want to see what happens, if I go where there are similar guys. We'll wait, and we'll survive. We'll read and argue.'

'What about?' asks Fay. 'And take me too. Dan, there's no guys similar to you ...'

'No, Fay,' says Dan. 'You're just a lily of the field. We'll talk of capital, and spend my cash.'

Gus says, 'You're courageous, Dan, but they will come and seek you out. They don't like guys that's sceptical about the future, if you just sit and read your books, or maybe invent – pasts, futures – when it all comes down ...'

'It hasn't all come down,' shouts Fay. 'You idiot! I follow Dan because he is my love,' and Dan says they're still searching for a quiet place, on sand, on ice, in mountains, where they can defend and say some prayers, it's not for Fay – he'll send a postcard when they're settled in.

Fay says if they won't take her, she'll tell Armand where to look, and maybe Gus has done the same, he did for Silverside and Frederson, and Apple too, careering down the slope ...

*

Armand the sociable – another chat ... He says, 'This guy, Gus Gustavsson, it says here, voyager. Lots of guys dying round him. And you,' he points at me. 'Some old guy on an island, the prophet on his rock, shooting young sprouts in the orchard. Classical reference here, and you to visit just before,' and I say,
'There's classic references all around. It doesn't signify,' and I tell him Dan and his computer state, it doesn't steal, it doesn't tax, and Armand waves his hands,

'No, no, it doesn't signify. It's only ether. Why, a coupla hundred guys all sitting round on rocks – that's dangerous, we all know.'

Fay says, 'You can't go after Gus – he's Inuit,' and Armand says, well, there's cruelty to animals – making them walk, then ate them, and I say that's more or less what guys who live in habitats, they do, and worse.

'Well,' says Armand, 'I guess I could get some guys, a gang, to beat it out of you – a thing I wouldn't do myself. Where'd the profit be?'

'Hunters, that's the thing,' I say to Fay. 'That's the thing – not of animals or people, but of stuff that's lost.'

Hunter

Hunter wears tan suede boots, black leather jerkin.

She says, 'Hmmm. Things lost and sought. Innocence? Frankly, I don't see why you'd bother. Truth? – well, memory seems a tiny province of that – if it isn't quite independent. When we find the case, that would set up some expectation – if you find a thing that's lost, you know things stick and slide – but there's a scheme beneath it all, just as it should be. And that might do the trick for what is real as well – a kind of point of reference. Just knowing things are there, though you can't see or lay your hands on them,' and on she goes. We nod.

'You're really sorting big things out,' says Fay. 'Though in the process we might lose young Apple's ghost, who's not exactly lost, but not exactly there. Or here.'

'And then there's Dan,' I say. 'Who's left, and lost for us, but not for him. And Fay's lost love – where might that be now?'

'First, find that priceless case,' says Hunter firmly. 'Where d'you think it is?'

'We've no idea,' says Fay, who seems quite tearful. 'Once it was, and then – was not. I remember well, the form, materials, the contents, even. But nothing, nothing, of where it went or where it is.'

'Of course,' says Hunter. 'There's no good if you find everything at once. That would flatten things out. Some religions are like that – something lost, returning, when in fact the fun lies in the waiting.'

'That way,' says Fay. 'You're bound to win – it's coming, or it's waiting.'

'You're very quick,' says Hunter. 'But not necessarily intelligent. It's what you do while waiting, that's the point. Fortunately they never come, whatever they might be.'

She goes on, 'It's like hunting animals – I know it's accumulation that you're interested in. Look, Fay, if you spend it all at once, it's all dug up – then there's no cute babies coming, no treasure for the gourmet. Deep in the jungle, lunch is fattening up, but you of the leisure class, dear Fay, you're only avid for the tenderlings.'

I wonder where she gets all this. I say, 'You mean that nature is like capital. That's dreadful economics...' and she interrupts – 'For you guys, lost out here, that's so. You've nature deep inside you, like a cyst: it grows and grows around, it's deserts, tailings, asphalt paths, and rockets to the moon – you can't get round it – just – it isn't sweet and green.'

Hunter points, quite like a dog, she does full circle, then, 'We often find things, studying old movies.' She settles down, as if a screening's imminent. Gus says,

'A continent! A life! Yes – the genius, Flaherty. My world. *Moana*, the South Seas – oh, if only it had been all that, then all these treks and punishments, the jealousy ...' and Fay says,

'Movies? Maybe those photos of us three, and in the background – is that the suitcase? What were they for, those pics? Dan's state, imaginary; the flight. My passion, my affair with Dan. It didn't make a dent on him.'

'What's with Gus? the South Seas?' Hunter asks. '*Moana*, smiling nature – did he think to go down there with cows? What of *Nanook*? That's more his thing.'

'It's all confusion – just some scraps, of music, movies. Think of all those films the Yankees made – about their cows. Who'd bear to watch them now?' I ask: 'Gus – he's bits of songs, and prayers, no doubt, animal this and that – he's like us all, too much. Just cobbled up of antique things, remembered references, all mishmashed.'

Hunter goes on, 'We find we don't remember things, where they were put, where they were lost. If we remembered, then they wouldn't have been lost, but better not remember anything, it gets in the way of finding things.'

*

Hunter needs straight thinking, but we've forgotten all of that. Dan sends a tiny movie, made at home, if that is what he has. They camp out in a yellow swamp – 'That must be Québec. Nigeria, maybe,' says Hunter. 'It's tailings, acid – yellow arsenic and chrome. No one will find them there.' Dan's movie's jerking up and down – in it, he says, 'We keep our arms, although there is no creature here, nor grass, nor bird nor living thing. We're safe. We shall survive.'

His head at times leaps into shot and out: he says, 'We'll shoot them if they come, and maybe sally forth. This, my dear friends, is for the long term. When all's come down, we shall be here ...' and on he goes.

Fay says, 'You see! what there was there, the mines, it's gone, and left some crap that's worse than worthless. Yet – it has accumulated, whatever lay beneath – gold, atoms, phosphorescent stuff. Dan lives, it's true – but not our love. There wasn't riches in the ground, when stuff lay there, quite undiscovered: now it's dug out and worthless – it is abstract wealth, it's Geist, like Apple, in the sky but still it talks, she talks. They have the power ...'

Gus is moved, he says, 'I'll go and join Dan. Get my gun, and join the warriors, at one with what is nature now, yellow like chrome and arsenic, but all the same—'

'No, no,' I shout. 'You don't desert! It's not that easy. You're a suspect, dear Gus. The deaths, the jealousy, ambition, frustration and despair ... They all churned in to make you murderous,' and Hunter says,

'What can his intent have been, to push and shove, eliminate those guys, and Apple too?'

I say, 'Intent? – well, once the deeds were done, I guess a quiet life, musing on the cold and on the sunny isles, and fantasies with Apple and her ghost, maybe, or other beauties, combs of gold are in their hair and lacquered sandals on their feet ...'

We wrestle Gus, he's awkward. We're astride, Hunter and I, and Gus is squealing, wriggling like a pig, a medium-sized one, fully clothed, awaiting death in quite the legal and religious way.

'Dust, dust to dust,' shouts Hunter, as she presses down: 'This way you'll learn that slaughter is a bad reaction to the way we live, our lost worlds all around in coloured chrome, and deep beneath the sand and mud.'

And down he goes. 'Justice is done,' I shout, 'Without the need to call the cops, or Armand, and explaining all conjectures, things seen, not communicated, might-have-beens and all,' and up go prayers for Mr Silverside and Frederson, and all the other movie stars and guys whose names get tagged off when you've left the cinema, who've done the technical and money stuff and driven guys about and made their lunch.

'Gus is dead,' we chant. 'Justice is done. And all he was – was malice, fear, or accident, pieces of lore and faith, his superstitious forebears dwindling through,' and Hunter says,

'He is not lost. We know just where he is, and if we want, we'll dig him up again,' and she's a friend in need, companion when it comes to thrusting down.

*

Fay asks, 'Old Gus – he's not come to harm?'

'Of course not, Fay,' I tell her. 'Look – he's off to seek out Dan – there, waiting for the bus,' and Hunter says, 'We'd not hurt anyone – though maybe disassembling those whose quiddity lies only in the scraps of culture making them cohere,' and Fay's impressed, and doesn't care.

Hunter has a turn of phrase. She asks me, 'There must be something you have lost, a past?'

‘Oh no,’ I say. ‘I remember all my past. One thing especially – that medieval town, the roofs like grubby toast. We walked the walls – at that height, we looked in the top floor of the jail. There was a man, staring through the bars, alongside – his dog, the kind that herd the sheep. A picture of a destiny accepted, repose, a stasis ...’

‘Yes, yes,’ impatiently she says. ‘You often talk of this. I’d hoped for something less resigned. That may well be the last, the only thing that you remember,’ and I say, ‘Well, there it is. Then, that will be my past.’

*

‘I’m very thorough,’ Hunter says, ‘Are you prepared to voyage with me?’

‘Yes, yes,’ I say, in ignorance: ‘Maybe we should dig up poor dead Gus – if people ask ...’

‘No need,’ says Hunter. ‘We know all the stuff that made him up – the thawing, music, driving the bus. We’ll reconstitute him – no one will know or care,’ and so she does. He’s not quite ghost, and not quite one of us: a character, quite a mechanical. We don’t know if he felt for Apple, so that we leave on hold, ‘Sex and love,’ says Hunter. ‘Always a tricky bit. We’ll leave him blank.’ And so she does.

'Look here,' she says. She holds a rope of amber beads, as large as turkey eggs. 'They're mostly plastic now,' she says. 'The flies inside are wire, with diamond flakes for eyes.' She puts her finger in, and pulls them out, 'This one is real,' and there's a beast, it's partly bee and partly homuncule. It looks around, and flies off, bang into the window pane. 'They don't have civilisation yet,' she says. 'And so the automobiles will crush them out.'

'Here, try this pot,' I say.

'Aha!' she says. 'Clay, creta – that takes us back to Crete: in here, in clay, there's bulls' pizzles. Now, moving on – there's sulphur mines, Minoa ...' and I say,

'Gus was keen on Moana. No bulls there, way down South.'

'Nor snow,' Hunter agrees. 'But we have lost the thread. That's what you need to get away from minotaurs .... You're muddling up. The Finn who wrote the song about the cows – Sibelius. A Roman? My, how odd.' She doesn't seem surprised: she twirls a glass, purple and foam – 'In wine, now, you find little twisted men, made from the roots, they carry grapes from here to there, lie in hot groves. A nymphet passes ...' and she leers and winks. Then,

'If you want the precious stuff, we go to India, where they make and mine,' and off we go, she holds my arm – and my! how those suede boots lift us off – we race like dust, like sand, and on the way those fingers poke inside the shells and free the tiny naked things we eat for lunch, and in the steel – we count the hammer blows, the sweat, the old-time fibres – all the birds and snails that lay down in the rock and – so they thought – they lived for ever in some girder in cement. Ah yes, cement – she takes that all apart, and here's the wriggling things and pensive eels.

I bump along, my knees are flat as plates, she skates, she glides as if she's made of air. 'Aha,' she laughs. 'There goes Arabia – cementata,' and I say, 'Hunter, you never miss a trick!' Oh no! We're into cards, and poker hands and croupiers and such. 'It's just machinery,' she says. 'It's gawky, turning out the fiche, and finding fish who'll bite.' I see her tweaking some guy's luck, and then there's tears ... I shout,

'Hunter – at least the platinum!'

'The mines!' she says. 'We'll go right down, into the core – these miners, they just fool about with gold and stuff – so down we'll go,' and so we do, she brings up stuff so precious it has not been seen, and never will again – stuff you can mould and eat and gift to women too, and 'There!' she says. 'I told you I was good!'

'Here!' she cries. 'Golconda's hills! They're made of diamonds, cast away,' she picks one, breaks it open, and inside, a drop of sweat. 'The sweat of kings,' she laughs. I say, 'Oh no, you're not a monarchist!' She laughs again,

'Much more than kings and queens,' she says. 'I didn't need a being born, that moil, incontinence, and then – the silly games, succession, invasions, all that sorry stuff,' and she looks me over, and she says,

'Well, going deep in you would be a waste of time. Those scraps and clips of black and white that make you up – they won't repay my work,' and then she kisses me, and I am bound to her – it seems a minute thing, a kiss, romantic, decadent, all that, a touch you'll see on screen, it doesn't leave a blodge of sweat or spit. But Hunter! Yes, she's good ... and off we go again, and now I hold her black and shiny sleeve, we race, we speed, and there are villages – 'That clan,' she says, 'will never do so much, it lends its money all within, and some are rich and some are poor – the best thing is – all rich, all poor, all right, all left – that way you keep the power.' I say,

'That isn't how it's done,' and she says,

'The power, you have to concentrate,' and so we do, we slide up glaciers, drink from valley streams, and all the while 'On, on,' she shouts. 'The saddest parts are still to come.'

'You mean Dan?' I ask.

'No, no,' she shouts, 'Dan's just another idiot like you, he wastes his life for present and the past. And future too.'

'It's true,' I say. 'And I regret. You know these material things far deeper than the rest, if I had been with you ...'

'That's wishful thought,' she says. 'My price is high, and we've not yet discussed how much I'll take you for, and all your life: regret, regret, for diamonds thrown away, a kiss ...'

Here, there's a plain. It seems it's covered with grey cabbages, but no! It's bundles, thousands of them, and she says, 'Those aren't collected. Inside, there's rags, quite warm if you know how to wrap them, ends of loaves, and such. Those were the Russians, left them there, never came back. Look, thousands of them, and we waste our time, for just one fucking suitcase ...' and we spin away, the bundles look like pebbles, strewn around, how'd you know if one was yours? I say,

'Fay has the idea – how the working stiffs created riches, and they went on doing so, though the machines moved in, and then it went on growing, invisible and strong ...' and Hunter says,

'Yes, like these clouds we penetrate, they're empty, you just push and down they go – a little rain is all you get, then start again – but in the sun!' And it is true – inside the clouds we see some lines of guys in caps and greasy pants, their faces in repose, and over there – 'Can that be Armand, in his uniform, sitting on a chair that's made of precious wood?' and Hunter cries –

'The wood that's in your head – they're pictures, tear them and they come apart.'

*

We see observatory towers – they look like Samarkand, the mausolea. 'Come on!' says Hunter, 'There was an observatory too, in Samarkand. Now – here's another wonder – see!'

A vast plain, covered – yes, in empty suitcases. It's bright, they're open, like the mouths of flowers, crustaceans. 'That's the Gaia syndrome,' Hunter says: 'They close up when it rains. The owners won't be back – besides, all the good stuff got looted. Here – take one – this one's for you,' and she brings out a reddish one. A shred of newspaper, says '-blatt'. 'Take it,' Hunter says. 'And take it far away.'

'No, no,' I say. 'They may come back,' I know they won't. 'Besides, it's wrong, the case is wrong.'

'You're squeamish, then, for nothing,' Hunter says. 'Forget Fay, her case. It's meagre stuff, besides – she'd sell it for a buck or two, and then it's gone. So what? It signifies for her alone. Leave her, all that. And be a Hunter – not for the meaning, but the inside. Inside's what you can know, and put a finger in, and winkle out some stuff. Leave! Up and away. No notes, and no regrets.'

'But – I could never be a hunter, good as you,' I say.

'That's true,' she says. 'But that was not the offer. Each of these cases has its value – if they don't, there's none has a worth. It's not to do with justice. All those guys that battle to the top, or you elect them – each in the name of justice – plan: assassinations, bombings, prisons. You're not there to take the score, and as for justice – well, "hohum" is the best attitude. Meanwhile – ditch Fay, the parasite. Up! your feeble legs – don't hunker down like Dan, in some polluted swamp and wait for cops with guns to flush you out. Fly! Over the world, alone, and free.'

*

'You see,' says Hunter. 'We found heaps of cases. It's the people who were lost.'

She's changed. She's wearing leggings of black leather, black culottes, I spy. A bra, all black. It's quite a spectacle on the street: she says, 'I thought – a quiet evening, you and I, to talk of how you can become a hunter. Some tricks ...'

'Maybe I'm not ready yet,' I say. 'My friends are waiting ...'

'Details, details,' Hunter says. 'They're all fine, the little things thcy do, your friends – the fear. My life, now, it's quite fantastic. I love every second. Movement, getting below the surfaces, and then whisking off.'

She goes on, 'You see, my nakedness, nothing at all to do with you,' and there she sits, naked, in a green armchair, across from me. 'I'm far beyond you. Satisfy yourself with Apple's ghost. Look! ...' and I seem to see us, flying, there the pumas, there the chrome, tailings of blue and white, 'You can't see,' says Hunter. 'Because you're trapped, all your little bunch.' 'Yes, but it's all as we say,' I tell her. 'Even the accumulation, soft and warm, a cloud, like the Master's beard.'

'Of course it is,' says Hunter. 'You can't run, so you must fly. And pry.'

'Yes,' I say. 'But you are quite exceptional. I've never seen another like you,' and she's angry.

'Well, you haven't looked. Have you? And if there were lots of me, you'd think it was a kind of robot, industrial. A fantasy.'

She puts her clothes back on. Her body has no mark of suffering that I can see. The clothes go on, it's like putting notes, the sounds, back in the clarinet. I say, 'We didn't find anyone who was lost.'

'No,' she says.

*

'You didn't find the case, the fortune,' Fay says.

There's Apple's ghost, and what is left of Gus, sitting there, not speaking. What could they say?

'No,' I say.

*

‘I’m off,’ I tell Fay. ‘Flying away.’

‘Some woman?’ she asks. ‘You’re no good with those, you know – you, “life’s delicate child”. What will become of you?’

‘It’s wonderful,’ I say.

‘Well, I’ll go to Dan. Make a last stand. With the Indians, this time – if there are any left,’ she says.

‘All you’ve accomplished here?’ I ask.

‘It’s always a political thing. People slip away, even while you’re looking. Now there’s no hope, so we shall be together, Dan and I. It was always so, even on the river bank,’ she says.

‘And leave them sitting here?’ I point at Gus and Apple, slumping there, two cushions on the cushions, ‘They look sad.’

‘They don’t look anything,’ she says briskly. ‘Armand can puzzle over. And now – where’s this woman, who couldn’t find the case?’

‘I don’t know, quite,’ I say. ‘People like her turn up, the mystery’s done when they arrive.’

‘After the ball,’ says Fay. She laughs. She’s not pleased. Nor happy.

‘The world is taking shape again,’ I say. ‘The pictures jumble back into a symmetry.’

‘It’s coloured glass,’ says Fay. ‘Just one piece, and mirrors make it balance out. It’s your illusion that it’s pretty so.’

Accumulation carries on, somewhere, I say, ‘Yes, chase the cloud, it’s warm, it rains down cash, if you are underneath. And if you aren’t, it gives you hope, it drifts around, it has its laws, its rules, but mostly it is there, on the horizon. Storms and dusk – they need their cloud.’

‘You’re philosophical,’ says Fay. ‘Because there’s promise of wild sex. Don’t take it seriously.’

*

I take Fay to Dan’s swamp. ‘You’re sure?’ I ask.

It’s desolation. Dan’s in a hut with guns. There’s no one else around.

‘The guys here weren’t of the purest kind,’ he says. ‘They read some books, and came, and then they read some more, and left. Last chapters always make you think again. It’s all for leaving souvenirs – those photos that we took, they’ll raise a buck, when we are gone.

Dan’s not happy, and not pleased. At last he says, ‘Hi, Fay. You like last acts?’

She says, ‘I love you, Dan.’ I turn away.

‘Why did you come?’ he asks. ‘A better reason there must be. You don’t conclude, Fay, you sit and wait for guys to bring your fortune ...’ and she says,

‘No, no, my case – it won’t come back. I never really had it, anyway.’

I say, ‘This waiting for the better and the worse – it dries you up. Think of poor Apple, not knowing what to say, and Gus with dreams and jealousy – both ended bad,’ and then I tell Dan, the best thing is to go beneath the surface, not to draw conclusions but to pass on to the next, and deeper still, and Dan says, ‘Well, that sounds like Fay. Or jungles. But with more discipline,’ and then I think of Hunter, friend and maybe wild card – but there’s others too, you might call friends – now they are dead, that Silverside, and Frederson. I say,

‘I fear for you ... The cops will get you guys. They don’t like bands who go to desolation, hole up with guns and wait for news about the State. For when it comes, you don’t survive, who knows if that is just and true, you’ll not find out ...’

*

Fay and Dan – they’ll get what they’ve been seeking. And it will scrape their bones.

‘It’s pointless, in a broader scheme,’ I say.

‘But there is none, no scheme – at least for us,’ says Fay.

‘It’s not at all, this thing, like what I’d wanted, but – I never thought of endings, only onwards,’ Dan says, – and there’s the truck with Armand and his friends, we see it far away – a man’s hand, raising dust.

‘Armand’s a little guy, a pustule – but he’ll take us in,’ says Dan.

‘Or take us out,’ says Fay. ‘Whichever’s more convenient, but not for us.’

*

I leave, and as I pass him, give Armand the finger. The truck has gone before he’d see.

Later, the cops won’t let me through – the worst, I guess. It’s not the battle that they’d hoped to fight, Dan and Fay. Or miss. Not in their destiny, for sure.

*

How generous they were, those guys, Frederson and Silverside, although it wasn’t good for them.

Justice and truth. Still there, still lost.

*

Now, to learn from Hunter – how to find her? I can't think – but now, remember, that she left her number!

Materials, to put your hands deep in, the fibres in the steel, ants in the rock, behind the painted canvas, the flax, flowers blue as eyes: down in the porphyry, milk and blood.

I call, she isn't there. And call. For sure, she will be back.

The Set

'I'm desperate,' I say. 'I've lost my money. My friends too. In jail, or in that place that has no exits. Comatose. Locked up, or in.'

'Then it's right that you despair,' says Max. 'And so, you come to sell your life to us?'

'Oh no,' I say. 'I've come to sell a story. In three acts. Real life's more expensive, comes on one long spool, not chopped.'

Max draws up tall. 'Now – don't tell me what you think of film, we get that all the time. Have you worked for us?'

'Not exactly, but a friend was possibly connected: from the Northland. A Nanook. They say his land has melted.'

Max couldn't care less. Nor in the end did Gus. I go on,

'It starts with this immense hole. The guys – this tribe – they've dug to get the magic stuff that coats the bullets, see.'

'I see a metaphor of hell and war – quite corny if you ask,' says Max.

'Then guys come, I guess they're missionaries – and there's strife among the miners, trouble coming, this way, and that. And all the time they dig.'

'They would. I guess they'd have to,' says Max.

'Then there's this dictator type, the good guys fight against him, pathetic though he is inside. And trouble comes, a suicide ...'

'Yes, yes,' says Max. 'A bullet – exiting it breaks the bathroom mirror. Brash, pretentious stuff. That's good. The protagonist – I guess there must be one – where does he stand? Or she?'

'I guess a kind of liberal: quiet times, no war, and just dig down a little, leave some magic stuff for future guys to find.'

'Yes,' he says.

'You're not enthused. Then, the protagonist ...'

'It sounds like *Metropolis*,' says Max. 'That kind of time. No one but us two will have seen it.'

'Forget that. Besides, it's good that no one spots the thread. The protagonist flees, taking a woman of the tribe. They find another village – and ... oh no! Here's another dictator, and much worse. The hero's spied and framed, the woman steals his stuff – and off he flees.'

'I see what's coming. Melodrama,' Max says.

'Another village, full of dictators now, no digging and no suicide. This time the lady that he finds, the snake lady, she sucks his brains, a hole right in the top of his head, and ....'

'No, no,' cries Max. 'Here's anti-climax! And what's it all about – beneath the shouts and cries? The bullets? Getting a raw deal? Victim without a cause? "That's how the world is, let's go somewhere else" ...'

'Maybe you're right,' I say. 'It needs some work.'

'Hmmm,' says Max. 'Those tribes. It's Africa? Or maybe tweaked from somewhere else?'

I nod, 'A civil war.'

'Worse. And animals – zero, all scared off by bangs. Ecology at all?'

'No,' I say. 'They're still digging. Cash you need today, or even yesterday.'

'You need three actresses,' says Max. 'And those don't come for love. They're all puffed up. The price.'

'Same person for all three?' I ask.

'An idea that's worth an Oscar.' Max is unenthused: 'It's the motivation that bothers me.'

'I have motivation.'

'That's evident. And everyone does.'

'Forget it, then,' I say.

'No, no,' he says. 'There's talent there, maybe, I'm sure. You could start – as an extra, learn the trade from bottom up.'

'Enough. Forget it.'

'Then again,' says Max. 'There is this kind of snickering. About capitalism, for instance. Yet – you want to play in cinemas – and there's the heart of capital. Movies: sitting in red plush, quite at your ease, some guy to serve you drinks. No hassles, just the good stuff, in the dark, no one to see – you pick your nose, it's as you wish. Live your life. What else you want to do? Learn the Koran by heart? Cultivate a friend? There on the screen, there's all the friends you need, no blebs, no acne, no requests for loans. Plots go on, relentless, dialog sets the tone. In fact – write dialog. Maybe that's your thing.'

*

The set's a complex. Here are restaurants, casinos, theatres, below, there's cells – for live food, bottles in the dark, and other things. Most people wear coats that tell you what they are. And there's more – it multiplies.

It's a city, a metropolis. 'Actors and the like,' Max says. 'We mostly do without. Especially the men. The movie's drawn on, now – some technique – I don't remember how it's done. We're back to origins, you know.'

'This here's Aspen,' Max goes on. 'These are her hands,' and he points out a guy with hands, pink marble from a Vatican floor. I look at Aspen's hands – the fingers end in nibbled shoots.

'My hands for now, but not for long,' she says. 'We're firing lots of people. I'll just wear gloves.'

She asks me, 'And did I work with you?'

'No,' I say.

'You've worked with everyone, my dear,' says Max. 'Even your parents.'

'The trouble is,' she says, 'it's all been done, there's nothing left. When I go out, the people gather.'

'What do you say?' I ask.

'They don't want words. It's presence, that alone. Substantiation. To touch. Like Hands, here,' and she scowls.

'Existencc before essence, then,' I say, thinking I'm smart.

'Well put,' she says, 'We can't think of fresh ideas.'

'You could try dying, then,' I say. 'Everybody's interested, but it's rarely seen from the inside.'

*

'What's the story here?' I ask.

'They don't tell you till it's done,' she says. 'It comes in blinks. Let's have a drink. Real drink. Real cash.'

The set: it works. Sometimes real, and sometimes film. All real.

You're odd,' says Aspen. 'Knowing odd guys, you say: Apple, a friend, Almond, an enemy. Strange fruit.'

I don't contest. 'I'm not odd – these names – crop up. In similar gardens too, you'll find. All of them, into truth and justice, all the time.'

'That's weird too,' says Aspen decidedly, 'Usually you think of those ... when you've nothing else,' and I say,

'Like – in blinks.'

'Well,' she says. 'We're not the norm. We make our cash pretending to be humans. Like swans. They're absolutely lifelike,' and she points – there's a pond, the ice goes in when you've drunk your drink, and there are swans. They stand around, and yes, they look at us, and think we're weird.

'Here,' says Aspen, 'This guy tells me what to say and do.'

'Aspen,' says the guy. 'Look at this silver cloth – drape it over. And – wear this gold leg-fetter, and the chain comes so – up to your shoulder.'

He dresses her, and she purrs into it and into him – the red lacquer sandals, the face-spots, blue and gold. 'Yum yum,' he says. 'This is a feast! If only ... Oh, how I admire that director, how he said, "The helicopter crashed, some dead – but I was watching Kinski" ... That's the effect, the life I want. *Tout pour l'art.*'

'You've lots of fine stuff here,' I say. 'And not just Aspen.'

There's guys who're falling from the sky; polished automobiles, Hispano-Suizas by the score, beauties smoking Gauloises, driving them around.

'I can make,' the Director, Raoul, says, 'eternity. Fifteen seconds, and you'll think it never ends.'

'He makes me live,' says Aspen, and she's a waterfall – a shiver at the top, a plunge – and off and down again, more rocks, and ends in spume.

'You're wonderful,' I say – and here's the camera, the metal stuff, the copper keys, glass screws in shining cabin trunks.

'It's true we only work in shards,' says Aspen. 'But we're a different kind of people. Livelier. The others sit and watch.'

'No one believes now what they see,' says Max, quite gloomily. 'The stories, all invented,'

Raoul whispers, 'We just fired him.'

'The camera – it has no in or out,' I say,

'I'd never have said that,' Max says. 'We invented mystery ...' and we ponder this, and all the while there's guys that run on by, firing off wisecracks, one-liners, Raoul doesn't seem to hear, and there are guys who try out guns, and guys uncoiling wires.

'They're ready to immortalise,' says Raoul, and I say,

'It's just like Elvis and his awful songs,' and Raoul turns slowly round to me, and says,

'The great man, the Director, didn't watch the bodies falling from the sky. It was his actor, Kinski, that he watched. Now, that's what real directors do,' and then he says quite dreamily, 'Ah yes, Elvis ...' he says it El Vis, deliberating, 'Those guys, they do it all with shamans in those parts, immortal, and the singing – they don't let women do it, so they do all voices by themselves – remarkable.'

My story. I say, to push him on, 'We had a guy whose grandfather ... he said he was a big shot in Metropolis. The movie, not the place.'

'Ah, yes,' says Raoul. 'I remember – too much running to and fro. Now we use cars. But yes, immortal too.'

Aspen says, 'Raoul used to make nature movies – nature's immortal, or it used to be,' and Raoul interrupts,

'Yes, yes, those two monkeys in the garden. The first words. Those creatures – they all eat each other.

Now, you take the Bible. Formulaic to a fault, but still, there's lots of treatments there – also a victim, fatherhood and battles, genocides galore. Then it all ends in fireworks and a song.'

At last – I'm in! 'Speaking of victims, Raoul,' I say. 'I have a treatment here that deals with them, it's not just paranoid,' and Aspen says,

'It's a set theme. Loss, victims – we've a warehouse full,' and Raoul is humming, quite distracted. Aspen says,

'He's a genius, he doesn't need an audience.'

I stare at her. It's useless saying, 'My! You're beautiful,' a million people say it and it may be true. Instead, I laugh. She says,

'Well done! You laugh and don't say that I'm beautiful. That's quite original,' and Max says we're all pitiful.

'Why do these guys all want to remake the Bible, or something like?' I ask.

'More easy questions, please,' says Aspen: 'Maybe it's the sitting in the dark, and waiting.'

*

Max says, 'I'd take your piece – rewritten, naturally, changed utterly, but you see, I'm dispensed with. Moving to another part. The world,' he points down some steps. 'The universe', and he points up some steps. 'Who knows? The present set – the movie has two endings – one, is uplift, striving. Poor Don Q, that stuff. The other – poor Aspen: a scene with pirates, porno stuff.'

I ask, 'Does Aspen know?'

'Why should she? Raoul always does it so, uplift upstairs, and down below, the trash. All mansions have it so.'

*

Later, I say, 'Aspen, I could insert myself, and win some friends.'

'Sure,' she says. 'Those swans. Their wings need clipping, or they'll fly.'

I say, 'That's easy, Aspen,' and it's quickly done.

'My!' Aspen says. 'You've quite the skill! You should do that for life, forget your awful movie script. Your friends, now – that was some apotheosis! I see the battle for their destiny requires they die, at least get put away.'

'Not everyone,' I say, 'is driven so. Poor Apple now – she didn't know the answers, and it wore her out. And Gus – I thought him a mechanical, but he set the goal – to march to Memphis, leave the ice and snow behind that's melted anyway ... Yes, it is true;

except for me, they all had something they would die for. Even Fay. Some were not prepared, of course, and some did not believe in what they did, but ...'

'You're the lucky one,' laughs Aspen. 'Even the good and bad cop Almond – he was for justice too, if not for truth. Though not prepared to die.'

*

'Of course,' says Aspen. 'I've made hundreds of them, movies. Your friends were fortunate – they could do it all in real time, life in first person. I've seen so much – the massacres in particular, though I don't take part. I'm in a room somewhere, and do some family stuff, or maybe a kissing sequence. Do people really think of that, when the guys are going round with guns and swords? And trucks. And trains.'

'Yes, there's the point,' says Max. 'You do so many movies, and then once – it's the one that ends them all, that says it, once and right.'

'You keep your eye on Kinski,' Raoul says. 'On the principal. The rest, they're replaceable, they do what they like, and can. Into the grinder, then another lot runs on. Here, it's not Metropolis – that was just a city, European architecture, though you didn't know exactly where. No, here, we can do it all. All history, all people. All places. All principals. No, we don't have Kinski, but we do have Aspen,' and he stands a pace away, and there she is, in silver and in gold, her body showing through and just a little taller, rounder, softer, than the life.

'Just sort out the story, we have warehouses full,' says Max. 'And often guys that wrote them, still attached, stuck to the pages, forgotten donuts,' and he laughs. 'It's just, Raoul, you're fixed on massacres and arks of God, and people found and punished – throw it all together, land it in the future, or on Mars, or in the camps, or in the caves. It's formula – the good guys, good cop, bad cop, love that's ended, ending, or it will. You're too much into what's banal, and been chewed over. Humanity – that's your fixation. Audience. You put the monkeys on the screen – of course there's monkeys pay to come and watch themselves. But in the end – all you got is monkeys,' and he laughs.

'Explain yourself,' shouts Raoul, who's angry, and inspired. 'Take the next step – and let's hope it's not some scientific crap, inventions! Give me the tale – what I long for: eternity! Though ... not if it means extinction infinitely. We need a body, central. Aspen here,' and yes, he kneels – 'An icon for the gays, it's not just straight guys fixed on her, and gals who gloss the fashion stuff.'

'My story ...' I begin, thinking I could pad it out and make it universal, even put some windmills in to give it class, and horses too, and even cows, but then Raoul says,

'Go fuck your rotten script!'

'It's not a script,' says Max. 'It's all without a word, before the word. Those guys could all wear skins, additional to their own. It's primitive. Another tale of loss and persecution. But, the motivation's lost.'

'The motivation's standard,' Raoul says. 'It's brutal guys that's insecure and ignorant and weak, and pile up corpses of some guys they've never seen. It's pitiful. And are we stuck with that? More monkey tales?'

'We want stuff that's more pretentious,' Max explains. 'And brash if necessary.'

Aspen says, 'But there's still who you call monkeys – you should make them grow, be serious, evolve. Raoul, you could take the next step. Up the tree. The secret movie. Something the future, only, will understand. Then, it'll be done. The film can end. Its destiny, its destination.'

Max says, 'I'd make this guy's movie,' and he points at me. 'Except I'm fired. It's true,' he waves his arms, a circle round the bars, the cellars, airstrips on the roof, here there's a Delft, and there Smolensk – 'This place is more compact than Babelsberg. But it's more chic than Hollywood – we can't remake "the woman of my dreams", it seems, and so – yes, Master,' and he points at Raoul. 'We'll make the secret movie, no one understands it till they're dead and gone, and then on reupholstered seats some guys will grasp it. Justice and truth – not fixed up there, upon the screen, but creeping down the aisles, into the blood and brains, popping like popcorn ... Revelation! Fireworks and a song!'

'Don't trivialise,' says Raoul, and he's disappointed that the secret's out. 'It's true,' says Aspen. 'Big things end up small. It's like the distances from here to other stars – they dwindle as our sight improves. But still – it is a noble cause.'

'Alas,' says Max. 'It's either all been done, or else so brilliant, it's never seen. And in that category – the never seen – there's rich abundance.'

Aspen is bored. 'We must seem disco types to you,' she says, and points her crimson tongue at me. 'I could be your little girl. Or boy. And strut, like a bright blue bird.'

Max says, 'Enough of that. This world we have here – must be something dirty, all to do with money. But who cares?'

'Aspen!' Raoul shouts. 'Don't horse around – or you'll go in the helicopter. We must be hard, not disco.'

Max says, wisely, 'Yes, if you want to be a soldier – stay out of the army. Want to dance – don't go to disco.'

We stare at each other. The climate changes. So does the future. And the landscapes – they revolve, it's a panopticon. We all know the other's story, whether it's been stuck on film.

Max says, ‘My story? A castaway for years ... Those goddam pirate movies.’

Aspen says, ‘My flesh. Does it resemble chicken’s, when I’ve not been dipped?’

‘A little. Yes,’ I say.

‘Everyone’s a story,’ Aspen says. ‘What we need’s a style. Stories – they’re just love yes and no. Kids. Pirates. Soldiers. Victims. A tear perhaps no one will see. Or care. Ghosts. Goddam – we need philosophy!’

*

Here’s Lars and Horst, down from Resources. Helping us with poring over – maps of the future. Lars is bully-fat, and Horst a lath, bronze in the face.

I ask, ‘They’re writers?’

‘Well, I guess they can,’ says Max.

Horst says, ‘First thing – your lives. You put them in our hands.’

‘OK,’ says Aspen. ‘Now, war? Politics?’

Raoul sits us in a Mexican bar, high on a coppery mountain.

‘Who chose this crummy bar?’ asks Aspen.

‘Here, the mescal’s fresh,’ says Max. ‘And Aspen, pass the peyote.’ He goes on, ‘The trouble with misogyny is this – you start with some romantic vision, then you're free to throw your bad opinions round.'

'Well, that makes us all misogynists,' says Raoul. 'And Aspen too. That leaves misanthropy.'

Down on the plain, the Indians circle round a stand of empty wagons. 'Those are Philipinos, mostly, now,' says Lars. I think of Dan, his Indians.

Horst peers at Aspen, says, 'Oh no! Your skin! It's like a grapefruit!'

Aspen says, 'It's all the lights, my cake as well,' and Raoul says – 'Stop! You guys are here to make the future something that annuls the past, not just be tacked on, and dripping blood.'

Lars and Horst – they seem offended. 'Well,' says Lars. 'We keep on changing things – the endings. *Hellzapoppin* – never ends the same.'

'That's not what I mean at all,' says Raoul. 'I didn't want no funny men sent down.'

'We're also funny men, it's true,' says Horst, with dignity. 'The future that's to end the past, not just to tweak ...Well. Hmmm. Maybe the universe, all that, it's just a joke, a game. Your spacecraft up there, dodging those black holes, the cats that's live or dead, depending are they here or there – although the Pope has said that relativism is a sin, though how you navigate with that ...'

Max cuts them short. I see that on his back it says that he's assistant to the Producer. That's a heavy task

– no wonder guys keep firing him, he bounces back – immortal too, no doubt.

'Hey, funny guys,' says Aspen, sharpened by her snack. 'You seem to think a joke's the same as game. The two are quite distinct, and if you can't discriminate – how do you set the tone? The future: do you stand to win and lose – or laugh?'

'I have no doubt,' says Raoul. 'That we don't want it all to end in rictus. Sharpen up, Lars, and you too, Horst.'

'Hey,' shouts Aspen. 'Any story does as well! I want to pretend to kiss again, and passionately too!' She sheds some tears. That peyote ...

'She's too hot here,' says Lars. 'We'll go downstairs. There's Riga,' and it is, the Baltic – full of discarded stuff, cold stew.

'Here,' says Horst. 'Try this cold milk soup, shallots and stuff. It's good!' But Aspen's sad, she says, 'This language here, it's so hard, even the menu – people here spend all their lives to learn to say a sentence ... This here's another crummy bar ...'

'We need more writers,' says Raoul. 'To thrust it all along.'

Max says, 'Here's Poppy, and here's Hannah. This way we'll get our story done.'

They're dressed in wool, and Poppy wears a badge – bread, freedom, dignity, it says. 'We'll splice in moral purpose,' Hannah says. And they, and Lars and Horst, troop off. 'Where? Where?' they ask, like sparrows looking for a bush – 'Shall it be Africa? Or India?'

A pause: we drink milk soup. Raoul in silence ... he has a story too.

The four return, they chant their outline:

'Spring in the Auvergne ... a girl, a boy, released from jail ... terrorists, maybe? they pop some pills ... the hills – they're quite alive ... the factory goes on strike ... people are rushing to and fro ... they make a movie, there's a satan with a tail ... up, bursting pop! out of a cake ... the girl goes blind ... the factory boss brings up the child ...'

'We got so far, but moral purpose – there's not much. The change of place and time – we want it cool, it may seem slack ...?' Hannah says and turns, asks Max.

'I'd make the movie – but you know, I'm fired again,' he says, and Aspen says,

'It needs a strong connecting female role,' and Raoul says,

'Children, children – hush. For this is not the way.'

'Poppy didn't write a word,' says Hannah, sneakily.

'I want to be not here, nor somewhere else,' says Poppy.

'Yes, that's the spirit, that is right,' shouts Raoul. 'Good for Poppy – yes, she'll come along. Benares, maybe, is where the inspiration lies. Aspen, have her take her woollies off, and put on something shiny.'

He rolls a fat expiring eye around, it comes to rest on us. 'You know, that *Hellzapoppin* was the last, the final, bourgeois movie? Few copies can be found. When the bourgeois guys got tired of killing – that world, it all went down. A bit like Croesus, they were – wanting everything should turn to gold. But it was lost, the bourgeois dream. So, they made *Hellzapoppin*. When you wake up, there's shreds and skeins all tangled in the bed – if bed you have.'

Poppy says, 'Hannah just loves her holidays in France.'

She is ignored. Then Raoul says, 'Away, away! What use to make another movie, when it's all been said? Except – there's always one that comes, after the last. Or else there's something new, entirely and tremendous. Yes, they both look much the same, the latest, and the one made after. They're just a movie, after all – what'd you expect – an uplift?' And he glares around.

Horst and Lars protest – they are professionals, don't bother with the history, how that's been made.

'Max! Don't pay them!' Raoul says.

'Of course not. I put my hand inside my coat to warm it up, not find some cash. Goddam! – but Riga's cold and drear,' says Max.

*

We're alone, and Raoul says to me, 'Of course, it's not really about a movie.'

'I know,' I say, 'It never is.'

'We've all we need here,' he says, 'And more.'

'And Aspen?' I ask. 'Is she right?'

'She gave her skin. *Tout pour l'art*. Give her short lines.'

He pauses, then, 'We need a forest, above Benares. I'll call the carpenters. All kinds of trees. They'll nail them to old stumps.'

A forest. I think of Dan. Avoid the jungle.

'It'll be paradise,' says Raoul. 'Of course, in paradise there is a snag. Always. Knowledge or ignorance – it is much the same.'

Below, around us – and above: scenes are, as they say, played out. War and love, no peace. I say,

'I imagined Benares to be by the sea.'

Raoul is irritated – 'Look, there's a river and a bridge. Temples too. Why the sea?'

'Just class. Cleanliness, infinity. The blue.'

'Well,' says Raoul. 'We could put it in. A process screen. And move the date – the 1930s. Ladies, English perhaps, with lorgnettes, who watch the guys, and lust for them.'

Some roughs move the things about: we have the sea.

'Why take this trouble over me?' I ask. 'I'm just an aspirant.'

Raoul laughs. 'You think about your friends? You should. That's what has impressed me. In the end, you cancelled them all out. The ghosts, the massacred, suppressed, or martyred for their love ... I've often wished to end a movie so, or just an interlude, wipe them all out, and have them in my memory. To love. Maybe I don't have the nerve.'

'Oh sure you do,' I reassure. 'My friends all reached their destiny. Too bad – but there's a resolution. And Aspen? Much depends on her – is she so strong?' I ask. It's clear I've doubts, but Raoul says, 'Aspen is nothing without her acting. Not "becoming other people" – but act! Wow! Is she good! Nothing from her, personally, intervenes. It's all commitment, all the part.'

'Max?' I ask.

'Insufferable, of course.'

We leave it there.

*

There is a great scurrying, hammering. Regiments wheel, guys stamp, sing simple songs. Maybe they invoke their simple gods.

'What happens to this, this set of lantern slides?' I ask. 'These people, dressed, undressed, with cinnamon on their lips, some waving tulwars, some chivvying their goats?'

'How should I know?' says Raoul. 'They're waiting for their moment, their story. Some will be deeply in to it, already, the script. Others without a clue.'

'You must know,' I say. 'It has to be you who knows it all. That's what you're for.'

'No, no,' he says. 'I just watch my actor. Could be you – your example, now, you let your friends all go, they drop, down goes your life as well – and then you pull, pull everything together, there they all are again! Yes. That's good, a good thought. Although it mostly hasn't happened yet.'

'That's what I mean,' I say. 'You know what hasn't happened – if it had, it would be quite trivial.'

'You need the story,' says Raoul. 'Then you can lose it all, and afterwards – you pull. It comes together.'

'It's all emotions,' Poppy, once silent and obscured, she pushes in. 'So I thought.'

Raoul says, 'That's why you didn't write a word. That's the trap, Poppy! There's no emotion here. Just lives, all around. Do you see any emotion? You must avoid that trap – at all costs. Structure, Poppy, that's the thing.'

Poppy starts to speak, and Raoul says,

'No, Poppy. You're wrong. Don't speak and make it worse.'

I say, 'Emotions come in with friends.'

Raoul says, 'Not in your case.'

Overhead, there's a creaking, Aspen shouts, 'The swans. Their wings have grown back. I wonder where they're bound.'

'I want a movie without the camera,' Raoul says. There's silence. We're all gathered round. He sighs, 'There! It's out. You see, I'm quite a shallow person.'

Then, 'What shall we be tomorrow?' he asks. He strokes Poppy's shoulders. She's wearing a shiny mac. He says, 'If someone asks me to join their revolution, of course, I'd do it. Instantly. That's not emotion, Poppy.'

'OK, I surrender,' she says.

*

Next day, there's cameras, all that stuff. No Poppy.

'I sent her off,' says Raoul. 'Now some sighting shots.'

I ask Max, 'Is it my movie?'

'Maybe,' says Max.

Aspen's painted up. White and brittle.

*

Aspen – she wears her silver sheet. Raoul shoots her as she walks slowly from us.

'It's a poem,' Max says. 'When there's music and we blur and soften. Of course – she's walking to the Ganges ... river of death and life. You'll understand the meaning. Yes, it clunks a bit. Often Raoul does a documentary, just for the cash. The movie – it could be yours, more likely his. But – plangent, that's the word.'

'Those facades,' I say. 'The buildings here – they look as if they're bombed. No habitation props them up.'

'That's heavy too,' says Max. 'What you just said.'

Then, on a level underneath, we hear a clanking – looking down, it's Lars and Horst – scything at each other: cavalry sabres, and determination. And – 'Oh no!' shouts Max. There's Hannah, getting in between. Cut down.

'That's terrible,' I say. 'She didn't make a mark, but sure – she had enjoyed her holidays. Those sabres – could have fought at Waterloo. Maybe they're French. Remind her of those holidays.'

And Lars is comforting Horst who weeps, though both have played their part.

'Goddam!' shouts Raoul. 'We've poetry that's cooking here. No noise, you guys!'

*

Hannah has been sewn together.

'Hmmm,' says Raoul. 'How'd we fit a funeral in? We'll put her in the Ganges. The last American casualty of Waterloo. Dead on the field of honour. A peacemaker – forgetting about history. There had to be a heroine, else the story would have stalled.'

'Trumpeters!' says Max. Several are found. Horst and Lars don't go to jail – 'An accident,' says Raoul. 'Or else we'd have to call your friend. Armand, you call him. Poor Hannah – she won't have a ghost, they wouldn't understand her here, there'd be no point.'

As they say – a brief but touching ceremony, and in she goes. Almost as large as life.

*

I ask Raoul, 'Is this my movie we are making now?'

He scowls. 'They say it's racist, and misogynist. And anti-capitalist as well. I'm not so sure we'll get the audience we want.'

Later, I say to Max, 'I'll change the script ...' He says,

'Do that, of course, extensively. But – remember, there's committees to get through ...'

'Committees?' I say. 'I hadn't heard!'

'Of course,' he says. 'Some hesitation too is near at hand. Some rooted doubts.'

*

'The trouble is,' says Raoul. 'It's not my vision ... A script that ends so. Death – it doesn't have the panorama – beyond the good and evil, truth and justice, that I want. It's just an end contrived, mechanical. It doesn't speak. But – why not? I could do your movie while I do my own. There's others, though, who may not feel the same ...'

'A test, Raoul?' I ask. 'I am prepared for any task you set. A sacrifice.'

'Yes, lots of those,' he says. 'Some sacrifices. Hannah was pure chance, and hasn't left a ghost.'

'She went as she came here,' Poppy shouts – an oration – as we drift away. 'In her beloved twin set. Martyr for peace.' Aspen has thrown some mushrooms on the corpse: her silver shift is tarnishing. 'I could do no more to show ...' she cries, and dries.

Without a ghost, without the hidden hand that tugs, brings back the memory – where's she gone? Hannah the obscure. No song, no dance. Into the river, and away, a leafless branch. Then, the sea.

'I was watching Aspen,' Raoul says. 'While Hannah was being edited away. You saw – Aspen ran a finger down her gown – the tarnish immediate ... black roses, black snow. The black – you see it in El Greco – just the reminder. The dancing in the dark, dark like a moleskin, covering us all, layers upon layers of us, into that black bed, the dark sleep.'

Raoul's far away, a greater artist than us all, than all our life plans, schemes to hold a scrap of memory that makes it all make sense, or rhyme at least.

*

I say to Max, 'I see there's always people here, moving from layer up,' and he finishes,

'Poor people. You can say it. Poor. Yes, from hot to snow, where lots of bad guys act it out. What you need's not climate, but the faith.'

'Getting a better part,' says Raoul. 'But then, it doesn't work like that. The story's set – or in your case,' offhanded, 'discarded.'

Gus the Inuit – he didn't know the names for snow: I say, quite nonchalant, 'We didn't see much snow in Memphis,' but I've heard the news, the plots against me. Max says,

'You see! You have a secret enemy. We, of course, were right behind you. Right and rewrite. Lots.'

'Enough!' shouts Raoul. 'Of course the trains run up and down the sets, they're full of poor guys, seeking parts – they insist on riding on the freights, riding the rails ... The only thing, that makes these sets like paradise is this: there are no tickets, not for anything. Those guys could go first class for free. But no! they climb, they climb, on to the roof. They need to find their destiny. They fall, they fall. Of course.'

We have no words: it seems fixed thus. He goes on,

'My movie. That's the point. It must conclude, and not be negative. Not be a monochrome, without a human acting there – not black, not white. Not promising, not judging.'

'I get you,' says Max, 'Spiritual. Not here nor there.'

'No, no,' shouts Raoul. 'No spirit. No quest, no destination, and no origin. It concludes, yes, but not a journey, not a thought, a life. It's not a comment on some thing. It's quiddity without a context.'

'It's like polenta, Raoul,' I say. 'You eat and eat, you're stuffed – and you don't want to eat more then, not in the future, nor the past....' He interrupts, angry,

'You! You are polenta! Where there should be sausages, there's just a hole, a shape, the presence of the absence. That is you. Your absent friends. Your absent personality.'

'Yes, Raoul,' it's Poppy, and she says, 'This guy here – look at his emptiness, that's where you should start ...' again he shouts,

'No, no. No nature, corn blackening in the sun, polenta! No void that's to be filled, no start, no end. No contemplation through glass eyes.'

'Raoul, you're losing us,' says Max.

Aspen says at last, 'It is your masterpiece, is all. My love – here, take the silver drape, lie on a shelf of rock, and dream.' She takes off the silver, imprinted with her shape. Raoul pulls the drape over himself – he seems exhausted. 'Ah yes,' he says, 'The sleep. No dream.'

*

He lies there, like a warrior. He sleeps, he dreams. The silver sheet takes on his form. I say to Max,

'The silver too – immortal, like the gold. It tarnishes, it blackens with a human breath – but then it shines again – the same with time. You polish it – and there's no trace, no stain. The little folk who mine, they may be evil, what they find is pure. They sing ...'

Max interrupts, ‘Careful! – in my world, movies with singing dwarves in silver mines – you have to exercise restraint.’

The Master, Raoul, stirs. He roars,

‘It’s Aspen. Of course! It has to be! She is the movie. Not strong nor weak, she’s sterile – there’s no story that is hers, no end, no origin ...’

‘You’ll see,’ says Max. ‘It turns to story in the end. Maybe you’re fond of her – that is enough ...’ and Raoul shouts,

‘Must I justify myself to you? Aspen’s a glyph. Quite isolate. No alphabet, no language, and no syllables. No meaning. There for ever, for ever gone – it is the same. No list of kings, no triumphs, steles, calendars, end or beginning of the universe. No written and no spoken word.’

We’re sceptical. Raoul says, ‘She’ll wear that silver cape – in that, she seems a cone. With a head,’ and Max mutters that it sounds familiar, it’s all been done: he says,

‘And shall she dance?’

‘Of course she’ll dance,’ says Raoul. ‘Everything is in the dance. The stars, the molecules – they dance. They never rest, they never start. So shall it be with Aspen.’

*

Max says to me, 'Although your idea's crap, it's not so dull as Raoul's. But – we are troupers. On with the show.'

I say, 'I think you're wrong – the nothing that ends nothing – that is genius!'

I think of Fay – her life a trundle till it sparks and arcs and drops into some black sea.

*

Raoul says, 'The test is this. You go through all the levels, all the sets. That way you'll learn about the business, and we'll see if you are suited.'

Off I go. The transport is by train, the good old Santa Fé. There's still the Indian wars, and then there's animals, some rare, some dinosaurs – but we rush by. And then I'm playing pool, and maybe dealing dope as well. A guy says, 'Here, you need this gun. It costs 200 bucks.'

It's all I've got – but I can hear artillery outside. 'You'll need it for your suicide,' he says.

And can we save these folks ...? and there's a line of them, all frayed – of course I save them, and this beauty cuddles up and says how brave, and we are having sex – an aeroplane, with crisp white sheets – she is all over me, but I don't feel a thing, and then the steps go down, I'm President, I won the war, it didn't hurt a bit, there's trumpeters, of course. But fortunes change – the guy who sold the gun – he's shot, you see the bullet slowly going in his eye and coming out and going in ... and now we're really down, we're sniffing glue, the crack is free down here it seems, but then a guy inspires – he could be Jesus Christ, or just a guy with cash he needs to launder or unload, and we're fired up – we're shorties all, but here we are, the final, here's the Lakers, all three metres tall, contemptuous, but we all hop like toads, the last basket hits the rim three times and then we've won, and we pick up our instruments and play the final tune – the best horns in LA, and here's the girl next door, we never heard her practising but – wow, what a voice! And now the beauty I had sex with in the plane, that didn't hurt a bit, seems she's my avatar, we work together, some of it's in wigs, but lots is looking in each other's eyes to fathom what we are. And now a guy is kissing me, we're raising kids, my! they grow up fast, and in the end they're heteros, so it's OK ...

There's subtle stuff as well – the raft of the Medusa: that goes on for hours, and semi-naked guys, their skin is peeling off, and there's a shoot-out – could be Fay and Dan, but they don't look the same, it is a tragic end, but we all learn to take it as it comes and not expect too much or turn to terrorism, all that stuff, and wearing beards.

'There comes that Indian chief again,' complains my avatar. 'He tries to enter all our scenes, I guess he's looking for his set,' and there's a party now, the chief gets off his horse, and wow! we dance and drink insipid stuff, it fires us up, and we hallucinate – there's devils in amongst us, they are dancing too, it's clear they're pros, you tell them by their horns and tails – those must get in the way ...

And so we kiss, that beauty, she's called Tanya, does some spying too, and probably she'll skewer you in bed one day and open your PC and find you're hiding cash ... it's time to take the train again ... The shells are going off, the kids are dopey in the doorways with their little bags, but here we are: Benares. Benares the beautiful, by the sea, and classy eating dives as well.

*

'Fantastic!' says Raoul. 'That was a bunch of real lives you had there. Of course, it's just a tiny part of what there is, you didn't see the poker games, the banking clique that saves the currencies, the guy that hacks into the military. It's all dull stuff, but must be done. The sex was swift and deep, you'll have liked that, it doesn't hurt a bit. I guess you left your avatar, that lovely gal, behind – you worked together lots, but now she's married to a guy you never saw ...'

Aspen says, 'I never wanted you – but, what a disappointment. You had your fling with that blond avatar and never gave a thought to me, to us, back here.'

Raoul says, 'The way you saved those nazis! Masterful. It's true what Poppy says – emotion's out, the moral law is in. She's one for nature's moral instinct, innate sentiment. You see, you act, you know what's right. Of course, it's Horst and Lars who write the tales, a lot of them. That's why the characters are all the same. Like us.'

Aspen disagrees, but Raoul says, 'Now – you see, I must get out of this. It's time to end. The real – well, it goes on, it has no choice. But discourse, narrative – no! Poppy. And no Lars and Horst.'

'Sure, it's ambitious, but to make a film about the void – it makes no sense,' says Max.

'No, no,' says Raoul, 'not the void – the real. To you, dear Max, they might look just the same. If your Producer shows His face, I'm sure He'd tell you one's within the other. Like snail and shell.'

Our faces turn towards the lights, the name 'Producer' fires us up. I say, 'Look, Raoul – I'll drop my movie notion, throw it in with all the rest. You are our inspiration – when the Producer shows ...'

'No, no,' says Raoul, quite kindly, 'maybe your movie's crap – but still, you've had a life: the usual rags to rags, but we can put it in the mixing bowl – your friends, more interesting than yourself, though still quite dull, we'll shine them up. I've lots more silver cloth, and Aspen – on a thousand movies, she has held the lamp that sets out rays of platinum. They are the struts that keep creation up. Then comes The End – and there she is: in silver clad, the lamp shines on ... It's time for bed.'

'Yes, yes, a thousand times,' says Aspen. 'Like the morning and the evening star – but now, I need a bigger challenge ...'

'That you'll have,' says Raoul. And Poppy mutters, 'Moral purpose. Lots of tears', but we don't heed.

'The trouble is,' says Raoul. 'A movie ends all movies – then ... they make another, and so what? It must step over, into the real, to be the finale there, the survey, the last word.'

'But still a movie?' Max asks, anxiously.

'Hah,' says Raoul. 'There's the real test. To make the real appear, and, staying in the real, sum it all up.'

I say, 'I knew someone like that – she did it, but she hasn't called me back.' I keep the name of Hunter silent. Aspen says,

'Well, let's get on. It sounds she got away, your girl, and now with Raoul, it's lights and makeup all the same. And Poppy too – her moral message – eternal, vapid, infinite. Who'd want to sit through that?'

*

As she walks away, again, Aspen looks like a section of a moon, the silver gown, all round, the silver clouds. I think of Mr Silverside, his silver side, the face, shines in the trench, the other side obscured, dead in the mud. His promise of great, immeasurable wealth.

'Yes,' says Raoul, 'I've pinned my butterfly. My lovely Aspen.'

He paces: 'Now,' he says, 'you all must follow me, and very close. Nothing escapes. We must put in – the Chinese working class. The last proletariat.'

'You're obsessed with that,' says Poppy. 'I can't feel a thing, not for obsessions.'

'It's the only thing in the future we don't know about,' says Raoul, quite patiently. 'And there must be crowds, that swirl. Some guys fall, but then they rise and join again.'

I think of Frederson, the big cities, living in specifics.

'The specific is a dangerous thing, for us,' says Raoul, following some prey. Max shakes his head, but does not speak. We jog along behind Raoul: he says, 'You see? A journey. We are in it. All this not shovelled in, but everything must be there, where it belongs.'

We do not understand. Aspen half turns, and waits for orders: 'Does she have a body? Aspen: you're just a cloak,' says Raoul. 'She's full of ghosts, they'll all spill out, like butterflies.'

Max seems exasperated, but he says, 'Raoul always finishes. There is the porno side. It keeps things going.'

Raoul talks of smugglers, and their dogs, of hotels in the snow. No, not a hotel, a palace, fine teak chairs and lampshades made of reeds.

'No writers,' Raoul says. 'We don't need them, their stories. Just follow me!' Again, he strokes Poppy's shoulders.

Lars and Horst, they hover round, clasping still their weapons oversize. Max says, 'Goddam it, hide those things somehow.'

*

Later, it seems it's done, finished. Raoul gathers us, he says, 'It was too much, guys. The plenitude. Everything. But it will do. For a little, it will do.'

How sad it sounds. How sad he sounds.

It's all been filmed – Aspen, the silver shroud, and her lamp, the rays: her back forever turned towards us. The crowds, the gas, explosions. There are elephants too, with little castles, red and blue, upon their backs. Guys firing arrows. Cranes to bring the creatures up and down. The scree, with bandits, their cute dogs. But – there's a story too – something about Aspen choosing between guys – one's a rajah, the other has a fund, or something like, and there is diamonds in between, and spies, and saving things for East and West, and Poppy says,

'The wheels came off this one! The motive – it's to reach the end. The gal gets right guy – and on the screen they consummate. It's Aspen's ritual – and she doesn't feel a thing.'

How sad.

'I had to tack a story on,' says Raoul. 'To get it over with.'

'Yes, everything is there,' says Max, 'And more. You feel you're in it, longing to reach the end. The mystery, epiphany.'

*

It's all a disappointment. I say, 'Raoul, why not turn it down, real upside down. There's crashes, risings, viruses. Unease, malevolence. It all goes down ...'

'Yes, yes,' he shouts, 'that's quite my show. Into the helicopter, all of you! Especially Lars and Horst – we'll give you all a credit for the sacrifice. Poppy, you too. And all those guys—' he points to whirls of workers, spiralling below, the elephants a-dangle, some tumbling down the cliffs, on to the sets below, the shacks, the piles of rust the kids are sifting through.

'I think you need some pacing here,' says Max, who's turned quite pale. 'You need a something strong, to cancel memory – the guys who watch, they've seen it all before, you need to cancel out, make everything seem fresh and clean.'

'Hohum,' says Raoul. 'What we need is what will make them sleep and dream, and when they wake, they'll want to see the show again. They'll have forgot...'

Poppy interrupts. 'But not the moral instinct,' and at once Raoul leaps in—

'The circumstances alter cases, Poppy, we all know about the altered cases ...'

'No they don't,' she says, defiant. 'Cases enclose, they cannot cancel. They are made of precious stuff, but what's inside's more precious still.'

'What if they're empty?' Max enquires. We do not heed him. Though he's right, and cases, millions of them, sit on closets waiting for the next adventure. Or they lie in thousands in some dump, open and looted, owners gone to dust.

We do the rewrite, Aspen loses love and looks, there's funerals until there's no more wood to burn, or soil or holes to stuff the people in.

'The End, the End,' cries Aspen. 'I can take no more! All here is lost – on to the next!'

'My love, my body!' Raoul shouts to her. 'Oh, precious wood – you never stale, you season,' and he turns his devil dog's eye on us. 'You guys – you think it's quite old-fashioned. Then, here's the surprise. It all turns bad ...' and Poppy says,

'There's not much choice. It's good or bad, or both,' and Raoul says that Lars and Horst – they must atone some more. He sends them scuttering up and down the stairs, the ladders, like California's said to be, stars in their gardens drinking hooch. 'Faster, faster,' he shouts out – their legs are oval blurs, and there's a squealing sound – oh no! – an elephant, it's down the cliff, and guys with knives go in to cut off joints.

*

I say, 'My movie? Though it doesn't do a justice to my life,' and they're all shouting round, and saying justice is a precious thing, you save it for the big guys, not just splatter it around.

Then Aspen begins to sing. It is a song of joy. 'They all can sing, the actors,' Poppy says. 'And there's always backing here.' And indeed, it's there, *shoofar rataplan,* eternally.

'I plucked her from a gang,' says Max. 'I guess you can't do joy badly,' but yes, she does. Raoul is rigid with excitement, he says to Aspen, 'Yes, yes, put on these pink gloves, see, they're shaped like hearts. This light-up tambourine to wave ...' and she does. Her

Hands was fired. Some guy strums while she climbs out of her Greek actor's boots and sheath – now she's in Indian costume, and she sings and sings, 'life's like a blazing gun / you dodge and duck and life goes on / and if you're lucky, love will come – and drink, drink champagne, tomorrow there'll be pain ...' and it's a disaster, and you love her, and Raoul says,

'Keep on, keep on. Now, we'll start the questioning. Sing, sing – we'll judge. Time for more endings, for those there's always time,' and on troop lines of guys, and Raoul puts on his pointed hat, he's Inquisitor – the first guys go directly in the fire – 'Too fucking eager,' Raoul says, and here's some more, they look like copper miners, and there's kids, and Raoul asks about the flesh, is it a metaphor? where does love go, is it the end in life? and some guys try to sing along and wave their hands, and others want the cash, and they too go in the fire, and Raoul says,

'This is the easy route, to ashes straight away, later we'll have a civil war, see what turns out, the good, the bad ...' and Poppy nods, but maybe she's just keeping time, and Aspen's fumbling around the breaks in voice untrained and wilful, and we all love her, and the guys go to the burner, some have had their cash, and some have written answers grasped in paper screws.

'It's true,' says Max. 'We needed another ending. And the song quite tweaks the genre.'

I think of modest Apple, leaping on the beams. So quiet.

'Join in, join in,' shouts Aspen, and the crew pretends. Then she says,

'Fuck! This costume's hot! But I love you, thank you so much ... Good night,' but we don't go, and nor does she.

*

Later, she says to me, 'You didn't join in.'

'You were in there on your own,' I say.

'That isn't it at all,' she says.

'There was the Inquisition going on,' I say.

'It's just another ending. Mine doesn't end.'

I say, 'Those swans – they knew how to do it. Off they went. Just like that.'

'It's nature,' Aspen says. 'What I don't have.'

*

'I love to do the endings,' Raoul says, 'but there must be heroics too.' Max says,

'OK – it's just another story. But it's "in the can".' I wonder if he's really the Producer, not His helper after all. So I say,

'Max: my story? I'll even make it into my real life.' He rounds on me.

'Get lost, you cretin! Aspen thinks it's duff. Plumb – duff. And so do I. Live your stale life within your skin, not ooze it out on us.'

*

'I thought we were mates,' I say to Aspen.

'What you want, idling here?' she asks.

'Same as you. Immortality.'

She says, 'I have it already, so don't bug. It's Raoul who gives it or not. If it's just the cash, you could do Max in. Or have Lars and Horst do it – they'll cut you in. Like Hannah!' And she laughs nastily.

*

I talk with Raoul. He says, 'Wasting your time. It's not about life, not about writing.'

'What then?' I ask.

'It's doing what I do,' he says.

'Directing,' I say.

'Of course. Shovelling it all in. Pulling everything together. Remember – style, not story.'

Poppy hears of this: she says, 'Morality, remember, and so no kids. No house parties – that's a bore. The *conte moral*. Maybe a chase. Adultery's all right – but have to marry them to make some sense.' I ignore all this.

'The cash you get from Max,' says Raoul. 'You'll borrow it against that platinum case you'll surely find.'

*

'I'll do the fat,' says Raoul. 'And you, the lean. But not here,' and he points down to a set far below. 'More elephants!' he shouts.

'If my actress is Poppy,' I say, 'there's a problem. She's a writer.'

'Take away her chair,' says Raoul. 'She'll soon adapt.' He waves me off. 'If they object, send them away. Fire them.'

Oh no – on my set, I see there's Hands. From afar, Raoul shouts, 'Get rid of them.'

I say to Poppy, 'No couples. Nothing domestic. No large animals. Broad brush, though sparse and pure.'

Poppy says, 'There's Lars and Horst ... They're cut and thrust.'

'Send them away,' I say. 'Although that's not your job, dismissing needs be your destiny.'

Aspen drops in: 'I might do a cameo,' she says.

'Everything!' I say. 'I'll do everything on my own. Though there's Poppy too, it seems, to fit.'

'It's enough,' Poppy says. 'Just me. We don't need other actors – males – they're all proud to be dull. Females are trained to sparkle. I do that.'

Not story – style.

Raoul says, 'You can always cut her out when you've done with her.'

I say, 'The first, maybe important thing, is length. I think fifteen minutes is enough. Avoid the long trudges – the Cantos; the Bible, always restarting with a cough, cars with bilious carburettors. Avoid too ... Parallel universes. Goddam realism as well – an affront to creation. Fifteen minutes ... a goodly time for inspiration, too short to suggest a prison sentence. Time for an urgent sexual flourish, a stripping off or girding on, a firing squad, a short march, a Declaration.'

'That's good, that's lean, all those,' says Raoul.

'There's place. Enclosed, a box-room. Dark, like a cinema, a safe, a cell – to store the jewels. Then – there's "person": we should have, I guess.'

'Oh no!' says Aspen. 'It's one of those space-fill shorts.'

'Hey!' says Poppy. 'I want the same spool time as her! What's a coupla hours? The past's so long ... I see myself as tragic, too.'

'Well,' I say. 'We'll puff you up. And maybe there's those swans.'

'They flew,' says Aspen.

'Old men making bowls. Tanks and marching, revolutions betrayed,' I say. And it is done. The future emperor, built like a wrestler, maybe oddjobbing as one – he lifts the bronze doors of the throne-room from their hinges, and ...

'The first part's done,' I say.

The poverty round here is wonderful: more extras throng around than in *Metropolis*. We can do guys for all trades, from all continents. Poppy sings. We can tack on another voice. We're in the future now. She dances.

Dances, twirls. She's clay upon the wheel, she spirals up, a cone, she drops, a lump again. The guys press round, she's garlanded, upon a wagon now, they bend themselves like oxen, pull until they crack. Now she wears a light-up gown, she shouts, 'The moral law! Eternal, bright, the only truth,' the poor guys laugh and shout – some have gold teeth, 'Yes, yes, join in!' they scream. It's samba time, they're wearing costumes – some are boats and some are swans. *Marche militaire* – those Roman trumpets squeal like elephants, impossible to resist, and Poppy's voice sounds over all, imperious. They trundle round and round the set ... the guys are shouting now, 'The moral law, the moral law! It hits the rich, it serves the poor.' My feet are shuffling too, it's Sambadrome we're in, and Poppy takes it from the top, the past the future, and my movie too. I dance along ... Oh no ... she can't be going to strip! But moral law's indifferent to nakedeness – the guys are not, they blast along, they long to see the naked truth, they egg her on, there's flagellation here and there, but mostly they are good as mice – and now she's naked, white as an almond pit – there's flowers and birds, and everything trills round.

'No, no! Stop! Stop!'

It's Max: he shouts, 'You fools, it's all precarious, this provocation brings no good. Discontinuity! That is the trick. You mustn't promise anything, Poppy, do you hear? These guys must be paid and fired, or merely fired. The movie must go on: specifics! – they dictate that when we've done this script, this show, another comes along,' and that is true, and guys are falling through the set, the floor is breaking up, the wagon jams, but Poppy's jigging on, she cries, 'Now I am my natural self, those costumes – much too hot!' And everyone is naked now – maybe I am, I don't look down, we're in the holy frenzy, speak with tongues, and birds are cleaning up the dead, they shred them where they've dropped down, on to the set beneath – 'It's natural!' screams Poppy, and poor Max is running round, enlightened, impotent, he shouts, 'You fools – at all costs avoid the natural – for nature changes,

changes the cards on winning hands, the spots drop off, the kings are knaves, the queens are whores! Distrust, distrust, and cash your cheque – if your bank accepts ...'

But we are fired up now, the guys are running round like water, the wagon's matchwood, Poppy shoots her lovely legs this way and that – yes, you notice – it's immolation time, the god – the law – is on us, better than tequila, better than mescal ...

'It has to end!'

It's Raoul. 'The movie cannot bring apotheosis.' And he thunders out: 'The cinema is finite. Tickets are good for one show only. Then you leave. You will not know the end,' and Poppy slides her shiny mac back on, the guys troop off, those that are left. And Raoul – and Max – they must be right.

Poppy's off the wagon now. I say, 'Poppy! I never thought! You outdo Aspen – you are quite transformed.' She says,

'You fool! That's my real self. The moral law is sharp and dour, it cuts you like a sabre,' and I am not convinced, but Poppy's glowing like a stone and hard as glass.

'Eternal and visible, that's what law is.' She is unyielding.

'You and Aspen,' I say. 'Always stripping off ... It doesn't bring back innocence, you know!'

I think of Hunter. Poppy says,

'With Aspen, it is just career. With me – it's the divine. Divinity without a god, without a presence. Some guy spoke of "awareness of the possibilities of life". There are no possibilities. There's law, to break or not. Your skin – reminds you of the beauty of the clothes.'

I say, 'It's crap. The cinema is possibilities. But you are not aware till you go in the cinema and settle down, and then the possibilities aren't yours. It's journeys to the moon, or into some strange woman's bed. Are you aware? Sort of, I guess. It's quite promiscuous. That's not the movie that we want to make,' and Poppy nods. Ours – it has the birds that tear, the wagons sliding off the marble, down into the dark, the trumpets crushed flat, into question marks. And Poppy, riding high.

I tell her, 'You can have peace – your tragic end's assured.'

*

I've still some doubts. I ask Poppy, 'You're sure this movie's mine, not Raoul's?'

'No, no, it's yours. All style, no story. Mine too, of course – my cause!'

'Yes,' says Max. 'You need a cause, and commonplaces too. That neatly boxes in the future. If there is one, it'll have lots of both.'

Aspen says, 'My cameo. Suffering, injustice – better if they're not personalised too much. I'll lend my name, and hover. Showing that I care. And breaking up the something that will surely come, a set romance – for you and Poppy.'

'No, no, Aspen, don't bother. There's nothing in between us,' Poppy says. 'Knowing people's always a disappointment. The first sip tells it all.'

I say, 'Of course, that's my view too. So many people are the same.'

*

'Poppy,' I say, 'you must do as I tell you. Or, I could cut you out. There's Aspen, waiting ...'

'Tell me to be brilliant, and to ignore you, then,' says Poppy. 'Choose a culture, too, to wrap the movie in.'

'This future stuff,' I say. 'It seems that fire and fleet, apocalypse – it's all discounted. Wanting too much – remember that movie where two guys seeking gold – they end up waterless, and in the cracked-up desert mud? Not so subtle, that, but nonetheless, it's all been done and said. The moral law, the loss, despair.'

'Then make the end a celebration,' Aspen says. 'I love the party scenes. Just gossiping, and standing round like aristos. No one on hand to check your story.'

*

Yes! A celebration. No crass collapse. No gods, no afters. Better than the dinosaurs – their last unruly gasp. What else, what more, can we do?

'You mustn't sound pathetic,' Poppy says.

Raoul's delighted, 'Why – his movie's much better than my own. Yes, mine ends without a high note, no final spasm. This is genius – defiance. Thermopylae!'

'And after, we just sign you off. No sequel, just your debts,' Max says to me.

'It's what I've always had in mind,' says Aspen. 'Being supreme, and all the time, so when it stops – that's all it's ever been. Supremc.'

We gaze down through the floor where Poppy's wagon snagged and sank – down there, is all the lost and found, the looking into eyes, betrayal and betrothal, fine thoughts and foul, the stabbing and the fornicating, abandoned urchins singing on the peaks, the crowds that run to handouts and from cops – on every set there's richness. Here the soldiers win a victory – there they're torched. The crooked lawyer wins his case – and there his client's put to death.

Lars and Horst say, 'Yes – that's the fullness, the plenitude. The odorous stream – it is champagne, we guarantee.'

They don't mention *Hellzapoppin*, but it's what they mean. It's in their bones. No one remembers it, quite dusty, shut down in a lockup. My film's a transformation, and I shout, 'No, no – mine's not funny, it's not sad. It is the set of sets, the case for every case, the memory of memories. Where everything is lost and found, and everyone is loved and lost.'

'Hmmmm,' says Horst. 'That's too dewy. No spine. Feel it deeper.'

*

'They say it's all been done,' says Poppy. 'The world, God, the lot – old cinema. Old America.'

I say, 'I spit on the history ... we're herrings, Poppy. There's no history – the history of the herring is something quite else: a history of eating. Us, not the fish. Remember, we have no history, no then, no now. It's being eaten, always. It's movies, every one is different, put them together, and they don't make sense.'

She doesn't understand. She borrows Max's spectacles, and looks into my eyes: 'No, nothing,' and she laughs. 'No, nothing there. No love from you, and none from me. Just eyes.' What can she mean?

'What can you mean?' she asks. 'But now, it's Raoul and Max, and all the rest – they flatter you. Just an excuse to do you down.'

Raoul says, 'This movie – all sounds terribly confused. That's lovely, what I love!'

I say, 'We could cram in – the poor, women, the work that people do – with all those extras, make them run and toil. Millions of them. They're all paid the same,' and I make that a question, one for Max.

'It all depends,' he says.

'Well,' I say, 'I came into this for cash – a lot. It seems I've lots of debt.'

'It doesn't count,' says Aspen. 'If we did the sums, our skin would shine like abalone.' That sets off Raoul – 'I'll find some primitives, and live quite close with them, and maybe find some hidden cures for illnesses. But – anger. That is what you need! Be angry. If thc boat is going down, then anger's what you need. I'll find a tribe, and maybe I'm their chief, and know a herb, a spell, that saves mankind, or puts it into lethargy, and when it wakes ...'

'Quiet now!' shouts Poppy. 'Enough talk! Let's roll! Let's shoot!'

*

It's time. I say, 'Yes, Poppy, now we'll sum it up. All the endeavour, all those days, the dawns that beckon, rosy fingers every one.'

'That's what I like,' says Poppy, rearing up: 'The fighting talk. Most guys – Directors – venture out, into the real, and hope it gives them authenticity. We – stay enclosed, here in the sets. An honourable demise ...'

'I'm in it for some cash,' I say. 'What's honourable?'

'Remember Hannah?' Poppy asks. 'Hers was an honourable death. And Lars and Horst – to the death, their fight. It is the way. The way of peoples, everywhere.'

'What for?' I ask.

'Yes!' Poppy says, and laughs triumphant. 'That is the hero's voice. That's Siegfried, raising the slughorn to his lips. What for? Those Greeks and Trojans, butchered in the sand – what for? they cry.'

'Well?' I say.

'For – a line! A joke, a scene, a twist, a naked shoulder, a slow fade. A lyric, ditty, villanelle. And then, a duel, a combat!'

'No, no,' I say. 'I don't belong in that.'

'Oh yes!' says Poppy. 'Nothing more is left. No honour and no destiny. The line, the joke – a zinger made up on the spot. The time will come when you and Raoul ...'

'Oh no!' I say. 'You mean Directors do it too? And to the death?'

'Of course,' says Poppy. 'Writers do it casually. Directors do it big, in front of throngs. And now the time is up, our species counts its last millennia – there's nothing left, you make your mark upon the shore, and watch the tide erase. And it is good, the death, oblivion – that's what the gods were all about. You go – they don't. And now we know they don't exist – well, work it out.'

I am appalled. 'But, Poppy, that's not style, it's story ...' and she says,

'No, no. It's style. Your life has been the story – rooted in repetition, the banal, same characters, same flesh, sparks of desire that fall and die upon the hearth. It's reputation, at the end, your immortality – you'll duel with Raoul, and ...'

'I'd better find that case,' I say. 'And buy them off.'

'Forget your fucking case,' says Poppy. 'All your useless friends, the plots, the wavering dialogs, the ghosts, the disappearances, the spits, the spats. You make your movie, then it's all between Raoul and you.'

'Help me, Poppy,' I say. 'Fence with me.'

'I did it all at school,' she says. 'And I excel. Though you're better at rhetoric than me.'

We fence. With rapiers.

'I can't stand like this,' I say. 'My feet, I'm like a mackerel opened.'

'Only other mackerel think that way,' she says. She pinks me, over my guard, and cuts a flower into my shoulder. 'It's not a flower,' she says. 'It's a sign. Keep your guard up.'

'Your sword's much longer than mine,' I say.

'It looks that way,' she says, 'when you are weak.' And 'oops' – she takes an eye right out, but screws it right back in ... Those wrists!

'You must attack, not languish there,' she says. 'It's just because there's so much blood, that I can't end it all, you're just a spitted mist.'

'We could use rubber swords,' I say. 'Or guns.'

'No, no,' she says. 'Creatives work like this – the foil, épée. And as poor Hannah found, the sabre tops it off.'

'Poppy,' I say, 'I don't see too well. But – back to the movie now.'

'No worry,' Poppy says. 'I back my warriors to win. I'm not that sulky Afrodite. Let's see, the scenes we've shot so far – there's me, the veneration in the cart. My skill in swordsmanship. Now, there's my big scene to come ...' I say,

'But Poppy, maybe in the end there's vortex ...' and she says, 'In movies, the heroes either die or don't. I'm one who doesn't.' With her foiltip in the air she draws a castle, peacocks round.

'OK,' I say, 'we'll take it as it comes.'

*

It's finished. We sit in our cave, looking at our paintings, as it might have been. What for? They won't last, you can be sure.

'They last longer than you will,' says Poppy. 'My! Those old movies – you can smell them from here.'

To me she says, 'You are not a Master. What you do won't last. How can it? You won't!'

She talks of a cat she had, or who had her. 'How angry it must have been, finding someone who feeds and loves it, and it must die so soon, so long before the person. When it's found everything ready for a long long life.'

'You're in the movie too,' I say. 'It's mostly you. It dies – you die.'

'There's no story, little style. Or – not just style: there's ME,' shc says. 'I'm a Master. I last.'

You have to believe her.

'Now we're in the future,' she says. 'We have to move around. It's about that – the lucky ones are nomads, hunters, a band. Nomads. Not sit in the cave, not knowing why.'

The movie. The last part – we, the eye and I, we followed her. Roads, all kinds of road, of track, chalk, clay, asphalt. Lots of sand on either side. All kinds of sea – white, red, yellow, black. She prefers boats lateen-rigged, sailing themselves. Hot winds. All kinds of eating – 'I'm hungry!' she says. 'No shopping, though.'

'Do you want to see your friends?' she asks me. 'Put them in?'

'No,' I say. 'They're in a bad state.'

Fay, like the angry cat. What a pain she was.

No memorable image. Or – all equally memorable.

*

Now, the duel. Raoul and me. 'It doesn't really fit,' says Poppy. 'Though we might put it in the film. It's quite anomalous, this struggle and its cancelling out. But that goes on, all over, we must honour it. Fight, victory, defeat. Battle. It makes them, us, better, so we hope. Not always, by any means, but often enough to make us try it over and over.'

'Just find the right combination, the right warriors,' I say, jogging her along. Such a fatalist – her having been a writer.

'Yes, that's it. We're revolutionaries too,' she says.

*

Raoul and I – we swing at each other. The swords are heavy. ‘Fuck all this,’ says Raoul. ‘We’re artists. They don’t behave like that.’

Poppy’s been hurt. Our weapons, waved around. She doesn’t speak or move, not hurt seriously, maybe, another ‘sacrifice’, a getting-in-between. *Tout pour l’art*, and Raoul says it too.

‘That’s old stuff, that’s style, but not in this scenario. I’m left with Aspen now,’ says Raoul.

Where’s Max? With his Gladstone bag, going round the lower sets, paying and taking.

*

Here we are, eating our popcorn in the dark. My movie, finished. Poppy finished too. So much for leaving, running off with her. ‘She’ll go back, be a writer,’ Raoul says. She doesn’t move.

Max says, ‘This movie breaks exactly even,’ though I don’t know what that means.

‘It has its beauty,’ Raoul says. ‘Did you intend?’

I say, ‘We wanted white, quite dazzling – and for the moment it is there, amid the snow.’

Max says, ‘You’ll be calling it “Pirates of Antarctica”?’

‘No, no,’ I say. Their reaction’s quite a disappointment. ‘We thought of “Here and Back Again”, but in the end the title’s obvious. It’s “Here”.’

‘So, you forswore the future then?’ asks Raoul. He approves of that.

‘Not really,’ I say. ‘The future’s in it. But you’re all – Here!’

‘There’s an awful lot of Poppy,’ Raoul says, and Aspen nods. ‘That bitch has quite upstaged me,’ she says, though there’s no malice there. ‘Though all she does is turn and beckon, beckon and turn away. The desolation! Was that hard to do?’

‘Don’t be deceived,’ I say. ‘There’s crowds – they’re in frame, a little box, top left, they multiply, they shout, we’ll stripe their sound on soon ...’

This could even be the last, the final movie. It’s all there, but subtly done. The showing’s over, now, blinking, out you go, into the light, into the dark. Depends.

‘Yes, well,’ says Max, ‘there is the thing. Your time is up, the movie’s done. Not the one you brought to us, but then it never is. Poor Poppy’s quite reduced. More work for Hands, I fear – he’ll do her body parts – so fortunate he wasn’t fired! And – it’s a risky thing, to leave the set, and roam around.’

‘We didn’t make it trite,’ I say. ‘With dinosaurs and vortices, and whitecoats saying we’re all doomed. It’s Poppy, going all around – a quite attractive gal, amid the empty places – those we found in heat and cold, and where the stuff had been mined out. Where the winds blow unopposed. But – there's no education there. Originality is out. No animals. That is the point – it's entertainment, rather slow, adventure too.'

*

'There's no other movie like it,' says Raoul. 'And now – farewell, farewell!'

It's over. So. They give it to me in a box. Lars and Horst say,

'You should have called on us for help.'

'Farewell!' says Raoul. Aspen wraps up in her gown, she smiles a little. Poppy's at her desk. 'The moral law was fudged and dodged,' she says, 'but maybe better so. And after all, it's always there, so why insist?'

'Farewell!' I say. 'You too, great man!' I flatter Raoul, and we hug.

*

I'm back, to where I started from. Nothing is the same – there's new demented, with their memory or sometimes two.

I have to see Armand, 'Dear me!' he says. 'Too many deaths around. And woundings too. We might take off your citizenship,' he laughs to show it would take time.

'Yes, yes!' I say. 'If it will help – remove it now.' He says,

'Some work of art, there, in a box.' He seems to want my comment on the film. I say,

'There's nothing in it that you see, about the poor, or tortured people – everyone knows all that. Nor about Americans, the only ones who don't need do the awful things they do ...' He says,

'Well, it's a privilege that you can talk like that!'

'I know,' I say, 'I love privilege.'

*

We watch the movie through. 'It's subversive,' Armand says. 'Your friend, Dan, he was subversive too. In a new way.'

'What do you care?' I ask. 'You're professionally paranoid. Subversion, now, – is spying to get more cash.'

'You'd not get much with this, your film,' he says. That's not the way to win me.

'It's the drowsy seed,' he says. 'From Poppy, her name, down through the silence, and the roaming in an empty world, no oil, no allies. Those people boxed up in top left ... And then – it's jumpy, and it's static. There's no story, but all's a kind of story, a history of what hasn't come about. It's inconclusive, and there's no linkage between one part and the next. It's pure subversion – it ignores.'

'I wanted it that way,' I say.

'There is a beauty there,' Armand admits. 'And there's an awful lot of Poppy.'

If there had been Hunter here, I think, there'd have been a plethora of her. But then – she didn't call, and I have said farewell – to all of them, poor friends, poor memories. And Armand says,

'You're right – why should I care? It's cult, is all, and there's an end to it.'

'It's just a movie,' I agree.

He says, 'Here, take your box, your Indian's head. I saw a movie once ...'

'I saw it too,' I say. 'This guy'd an Indian's head he'd cut, and carried it around ...'

'Another guy took it, threw it away,' says Armand.

'It wasn't delicate,' I say, 'the way it went,' and Armand says,

'That's an American thing you've said,' as if to lead me on. 'You're quite a Bluebeard! All those women, some live, some dead. Now Poppy, run right through.'

'Behind the partition, they are all alive,' I say. 'Especially Poppy. I wish I had an analytic mind like you. Sort people out, like that.' I ingratiate myself. It does not catch. He says,

'If you had had an analytic mind – you wouldn't lose your fortune, gone on to make a movie.'

'You know almost everything,' I say. 'You know what subversion is, how far it carries.'

I want that information, want to know. He doesn't give.

'Everything will be all right,' he says. 'Don't worry. Everything, just fine. Here – see this parure? Make me an offer and it's yours.' I think, 'It isn't yours.' He says, 'Buy it for Poppy, have it hide those holes you put in her.'

He knows these things, departures, arrivals, people also. Is it just knowledge, or is there action too? I say, 'People are real and brittle – places are not.'

Armand understands – 'You want me to cancel citizenship, then?'

After the sets, there's no more country. Max and his bag, those extras, coloured like the seas – black, red, yellow, white: infinity.

'It's done,' says Armand. 'You're no person, in no place. But – movies is so *vieux chapeau*, my friend. That, you'll regret. Too bad, your crimes, done and to come – they can't be taken out. They're on the books. Dan said "no surrender". That was a stupid thing to say – a provocation'.

*

Poppy's waiting for me. Just like Armand said.

'I'm here for my money,' she says.

'You heard Max,' I say. 'We broke even.'

'Broke I hear,' she says. 'The rest – I don't understand.'

Step outside your world – your country, they call it – and you two Directors, you're two scholars, with two courtesans. At ease, beneath a tree. The artist draws you in, like that.

'It's good to be with you, Poppy,' I say. 'Though I guess those swords ... you must be full of holes, we can see right through.'

'Money,' she says.

'You need to understand,' I say.

'I know about all that,' she says. 'Max is from Hong Kong. He talks a lot, and it's all secret. Raoul's from Vietnam,' she says.

So what? She goes on, 'It explains how they talk about my pay. And Aspen and I, we're just two ordinary ...' She leaves it dangle. Ordinary what? Divas? Chinese? Courtesans?

She says, 'I liked the bits about the swans.'

'Good,' I say. 'That movie! It was full of best bits.'

'And I was the star,' she says.

'You are the star,' I say.

'At least you know that,' she says. 'And now we can have more adventures. Out of Armand's way, and all that dull stuff. Keep your mouth shut, and seem to talk a lot. Beyond Armand and those odd film guys you used to come across. Micawber!' And she laughs: 'Scottish?'

'Well,' I say. 'It's all our world. Big inconclusive cities. Rackety hells. All the rage.'

'The rage,' and she laughs again. 'Dan and Fay – what a terrible end.'

'Don't tell me,' I say. 'Don't mention them.'

'Then there were your two mechanicals. The gymnast and the cowboy. They didn't do too much. Terrible endings too. Maybe your friends didn't like you specially.'

'It would not be a surprise,' I say. 'And Aspen wanted to block everything.'

Poppy says, 'She's made for sacrifice. She's a pirate ship.'

I say, 'It doesn't fit – pirates fight to the last.'

'Yes,' says Poppy briskly, 'that's what she does, and I do as well. Even if there's no cash.'

'I owe you, Poppy,' I say.

'Yes, you do,' she says. 'A lot. But have no fear, for you, your friends, the crimes ... Armand is a special cop, high up that tree. Contingent crimes don't bother him. He searches out ideas. Besides, if you did bad, then you harbour all their ghosts. They visit, without rancour. Besides, who is to judge – think of the complicit ones, that wriggly mass, the decent folk. They even vote for wars.'

'Poppy, you're right,' I say. 'There should be lots of ghosts for everyone. Besides, it's not the people and the wars I care about – it's to be on the outside. Not rhetoric within – but style.'

'Yes,' she says. 'That's why you should have made more movies. Lots of them, and paid the bills.'

Poppy encourages. Hunter didn't – she doesn't even have a ghost. Poppy says,

'You're nowhere, with emotions and your theories. It's just the best to know – there is a right and wrong. A right way and a wrong way. And leave it there.'

I leave it there, at that. You can't go further.

'Hunter'

'Look,' says Poppy. 'I'll be Hunter. She doesn't call. And she knew the right way, so you say. If she calls, I'll be someone else. It's my profession now. As for right ways and right – that's quite enough. You know as much as anyone, so no more about it.'

'Yes!' I say. 'Hunter went to the heart of things, the origins.'

'Well – which was it? Endings or starts? If she's in our movie, she'll be a dragonfly.'

Poppy makes a good Hunter. She says, 'We don't need put it down as film. We'll visualise. And I've scores to settle. Places, people. Your ghosts – we'll use all those. Elvis – he can do the sound, he's always in our ears. Silverside and Frederson – they're the two good fairies, bringing wealth and detail, crowds and their bosses – yes, you need all those, though they were clumsy with things in the end. Something always turns up – that is life, my dear.'

'Yes!' I say, convinced. 'You can be Hunter.'

Poppy puts her head briefly on my shoulder.

'Believe in me! Treasure me, trust me!' she says. 'I can cover the world. Shop and pray! Soft and hard! Defend, attack – they come out much the same. Settle the scores – with love and justice!'

She is an arbiter superb.

She seeks an accompaniment. Seeks a person, for the moment, me – complicit deeper than sex, but the project is her own, exclusively. Hunter, though, she was all self-assertion, not settling scores, or having plans. Poppy says,

'I want no feeling that doesn't have a consequence. Leading to action, that can have good outcomes.'

I say, 'You're saying you want no memory that isn't your whole life. One memory. Dementia. For you, Poppy, emotion's just obsession.'

'Yes, that's right. Of course.'

She stares at me: ‘You’re up and down. Not dark at all. You’re Vogue, you’re fashion. Spend some years, making those little telephones on the line. Toughen you.’

‘Everywhere, that’s women’s work,’ I say.

‘Complaining’s even more bourgeois than the rest,’ she says.

Later, she says, ‘I want real power. May cause real hurt.’

‘Yes, I’ve seen it coming,’ I say. ‘But – your inner life? You were a writer.’

‘I’ve never understood that stuff,’ she says. ‘Lots goes on inside for everyone – just life of the simplest boring kind. I used to give the dialog – Hannah wrote it down. We talked, and that was it.’

In this bar, where we sit – ‘I can’t wait,’ says Poppy. ‘To be about the world, righting wrongs and wronging rights,’ – there’s a guy alone, composing. Obituary, for his girl. Close by, a table full of fates and fairies, drinking Armagnac.

‘I have to write her farewell note,’ says the guy. ‘And when I’m done we weight her, put her in the river, and that’s done as well. We can’t decide – face down – that seems the pious way. Face up – is glory to the sun, all that.’

‘Why can’t she do the note herself?’ asks Poppy.

‘This Armagnac,’ the waiter says, ‘is thirty-five years old.’ He slides behind a pillar, takes a swig.

'She says she has no inner life, and so I'm left to set down those last thoughts. She's reached her end,' says the guy. 'We'd years together. Now we won't.' He shows us what he's done. It's all about him.

'That is life,' says Poppy. 'When it starts, they give your name, but at the end – it's credits, not for you, but for the drivers and the caterers. That is right and just. And if you've taken off your clothes or taken bullets, and the guys forget your name, that is too bad. There is no going back.'

The lady rises as we leave, waves her glass: the guy, I see, is writing into nature now – 'the celandines ... a hatch of maybugs,' a mistake, I think. The lady's tall and overloaded. Poppy says, 'When you design a human, it's their line you have to watch. The frills and pompoms – no! Cut them out! But on the whole, I find it bracing, ending so. Quite exhilarating. Into the river when you've done, like Hannah. Now – to our business.'

'Not harming Max and Raoul?' I ask.

'Of course not. They owe me. They sit in ruined empires – Raoul's is long gone. Now, he's amidst those sets, like the cliffs of California, tumbling down to rifts. Poor Max, his empire! What a fraud! Making things and stuffing cash in banks! Think of it – we could have sat there, on the scroll, me and Aspen, wily tarts, and you and Raoul, not a care in those tall ivory pates. Me – I don't have empire in my bones. That realism, the sense of place they talk about, and history

– it's all to do with empires. You smell the reek from here. I'm me, I'm not my movie! I'm who I am, no thanks to anyone!'

Yes, she does Hunter well: I say, 'The detail ...' and she shouts, 'And fuck small countries too!' and up she leaps, on to a parapet that overhangs the river, and we watch the water at its work.

'I'll be a cult,' she says. 'Not like that woman in the flow.'

'Like Elvis?' I ask. 'But a better shape. We weren't believers when we went to Memphis, but animals were sacrificed.'

'Another metamorphosis or two, to set me up ...' she says. 'No hurry, though. Of course, I love the good and hate the bad. Now, let's get on. It's Aspen lets the others draw conclusions – they show the movie about Aspen, they don't show Aspen's movies.'

They don't show Poppy's either, but it doesn't interest, it doesn't matter. Consolation and greasepaint – those swarm out, however tough she'd like to seem.

'I see there's anarchists,' she says. 'I'll help them smash things up. And then I'll help the moderates to smash the anarchists.'

'Yes, Poppy, you can do all that,' I say. 'But no one really cares.'

'Of course they care,' she says, angry and amused.

'I'm not sure your way is my way,' I tell her. 'The body. This aesthetic stuff. The stripping off. Regenerating novelty – it's not what I started from.'

'You took the cash from Silverside,' she says. 'You made the movie. You didn't follow Fay and Dan. One thing leads on, then it's the next. You never broke the chain.'

She holds the chain. Armand maybe waits, he maybe holds the chain as well, and hopes for revelations, to be against or for.

'Of course,' I say. 'It's just ... perhaps addiction, I love that smell of musk and acetone ... The ratty scent.' All I have been. She doesn't understand, or maybe she is set upon her way.

She says, 'You're with me now, like it or not. You started, so you have to reach the end.' She peers at me, as if she wants to film my skin. 'I need attachment, to a person. I don't think it could be you. But – I can deal with feelings too. I'd hate frequenting some caring circle, hugging other psychopaths.'

She's a galley, beautiful, without her slaves, her oarsmen: becalmed – her lips, painted blue, against an ocean red in stripes. Silent, the drum that gives the beat.

I must sell Poppy, have her make a fortune too.

Here's a guy, the overhearing kind. 'We need a kind of no-place, no-state,' I say. 'Where the sensibility's opposed to movie-making, but they watch them just the same.'

The guy, Yves, says, 'A little emirate, perhaps? Petulant, but future-bound?'

*

'This guy, Yves,' says Poppy: What's his story?'

'None,' I say. 'He wants to make you happy. Reach your end. Your goal, that is.'

'Yes,' she says. 'Everyone has goals, some turn out to being ends. Apple was the only one who had an end without a goal. Mine is clear. There is the moral law, indifferent. Friends, bringing memories. There's those guys – Raoul, making another movie and another one, and when he's reached perfection, down he'll go – decline and having medals. Aspen – more shows, like warts upon a salamander. But me? What can I have, what can I want? I can't go forward, there's no going back.'

'Well,' I say, 'even going forward's quite an inescapable thing,' I try to cheer her. She says,

'Many queens are buried on the shore. Yes, I'd like that. Only – who's to bury me? And sing? Not you!'

'Who says you're queen?' I say. 'That's first to be achieved. No politics, no economics. Novelty's the thing.'

Yves says, 'You guys – just stepped off the screen? I love your epics, the vendettas, the slave guys doing stunts.'

'No, no,' says Poppy. 'I'm quite real. We both are real as real.' She pirouettes. 'You – Yves! – away with your suggestions!' and she shouts: 'No air-conditioning – that brings dementia to the world. A cop-out. And no emirates!' He says,

'Without offence! An emirate is just a place for contemplation.' Poppy shouts,

'That's a bad place! The worst thing. Hunter knew! The evil scene, two guilty guys, alone, in some agreeable room. Some other guy, invisible, up high somewhere, his plan, coming about on both their heads.'

*

And here we are. Back in a place, a room, quite like where I set out. A tower, the twisting streets below, and over there, the country, a scrub of aloes. Homes – they're all the same.

'Yes,' I say. 'It's home.'

Poppy stares at me some more: 'The trouble is,' she says, 'your eyes. They looked into that lens, they made the story. The style, you call it. What they saw's your law, your future. Specious the logic, yours alone the reasoning. And us – the failed princesses. Things you can't see – there's women: and there's work. You're infantile, and idle too. It's all about your eyes. Mine – they see it all quite different.'

It's true. No doubt at all. Beyond the film: – there, you don't find naturalness, and death. Real things will be much tougher, not filmic.

'You haven't understood at all,' she says, exasperated.

Yves is ever at the door, he hovers. Poppy points at him and says to me, 'You have the trick of gathering knowalls – in the end they fall in holes. That's not women's justice. That's not work!'

'I know, Poppy,' I say. 'It's the culture, it's convention. A turn of the spool never abolishes repetition. I'm stuck in it. What I dream up ... the same mash they have always made in barns—'

'No use, ingratiating yourself with me ...' she says.

Yves fidgets as we bicker.

'Come, Yves,' says Poppy. 'What potent fruit this time? What knowledge that makes us drudge to doom and worse?'

Yves says, 'I saw your movie, it's a cult. There's nothing more to say. It told nothing that I need to know. But it was full, like an addled egg. Like some guy who tells you his tale in the street, then you never see him again. Gives his lineage. What you should eat. If you displease, he'll set his demons on you. Lots of Poppy, of course. I mustn't say she's beautiful.'

I'm flattered and disappointed. Poppy says,

'Exactly! They showed me dominant.'

Yves tells his tale,

'My life so far – is getting things to people who shouldn't have them.' He opens up his face: it's like a leather wallet, emptied, kicked on a pavement somewhere. He turns its full moon on us: empty and open.

Selling things, and travelling. Hotels, and sometimes running out – leaving a suitcase.

'You remember Fay?' Poppy asks me.

'Of course – nothing specific. A bad end. Losing that case,' I say.

'Well,' Poppy goes on. 'You must remember something – from earlier?'

I say, 'When I was very young – they said they'd killed a trooper – he stole a coat from someone on the battlefield. The well, I remember – and the pole you used to swing the bucket up. The potatoes – all floury, like dust.'

'There you go, then,' says Yves. 'People flee the battlefield. I'd do it myself, though I don't steal, I sell. I'd take you to the emir – his place is full of opportunity. Remembering too much, especially people – it grinds you down. You travel lightly ...' on he goes.

He takes us to this place. There's no outside. It's all hotel. Most things are run by Indians. Yves says,

'I have to sell them stuff, all the big cheeses here. The Emir's relatives are into film. With Poppy tagged along, I make some deals – and no, they didn't see your show, enough it is that Poppy bears the chrism ...'

I sit, down in the hotel cinema. No popcorn, but a festival of Raoul's films. Here's nature – my! how those animals just love to eat each other, at the end there is one left. It takes an hour for that big snake to – yes, there go the last of that giraffe's neat hooves, its tail remains outside. Then there's a short on ghosts – no actors here, just furniture a-jiggling. There's comedies, though you don't laugh. I think of Gus – a guy like him, he comes and goes in everything – he drives the cars, he opens doors, he winks and goofs around. I think of Apple, and her ghost that squats upon my shoulder, whispers in my ear. Then there's a feature – classy too, it's called *Les mains d'Aspen.* There goes Hands, a major role, and Aspen, mostly from behind, until the helicopter cash – there go her kids, and husband, lovers too – and Hands is up in air, and Aspen screams, she's like Elektra – and she takes a knife – she's Clytemnestra now – there's the last lover, maybe the pilot, scuttering down the slope. Here she is again, she wipes the blade, and that's the end. A closeup of her Hands.

*

'What's Yves selling?' I ask Poppy.

'Stuff in tubes, he says is trees,' she says. 'Those movies – my, they crawl up your nose! It's meaty stuff. Raoul – he spares no one who's around. You notice, there's no dialog, it's gestural. Just Aspen, singing: "the wind obliterates my footprints / as with my last journey I rejoin my love ..." You're lucky,' Poppy says, 'You have no love. Yves – he sells no dreams, like what I guess you'd hope. Your Silverside. Or revelation, like that Frederson. At best, there's trees. How this place needs something like!'

We stare down. There's a great roundabout, big motors crawling round. Poppy says, 'It's not our fight.' The Indians bring us milky tea. Camel milk, for sure. I say, 'It must be hot outside,' they crack a smile, they recognise an idiot from afar.

Crowds gather: 'They're like our extras,' Poppy says. 'Always hopeful. Too bad, about the future – our movie hadn't one – just me.'

'Crowds in the future – they're a great expense,' I say. As we watch the swirls below, Poppy rests her head, quite briefly – on my shoulder. As Hunter would not do. Where Apple sat: truncated sprite.

I say, 'Well, Poppy, you and I – we have a kind of sympathy.'

She says, 'You know – I see you rather as, well ... a bad hand. Improbable to make you win.'

Yves rushes in, he looks down at the guys – 'Trees, trees, and ever more,' he says. 'Let's get out now – I hate a crush.'

'Hunter would have left by now,' says Poppy, as we run.

'Which crowd, which way?' I shout – converging wedges, summoning the future.

'My trees! The trees!' says Yves, quite out of breath. It's true! They're trees, still wrapped and propped ... Of course! Dan said the trade in serious things is done by states. Trees is just trees.

Up there, in the hotel, the Indians look down and on.

'We're running for our future too,' says Poppy. 'It will take the finished movie till we know if danger's on all sides,' and Yves exclaims, 'The movie says we all escape!' and Poppy says,

'No, no, we need a sacrifice. Not everyone will make it past the present ...' and we quite lose heart.

I think, 'Oh Fay, where are you now?' and that is desperation, for to be where Fay has gone, no one would wish.

We hide behind some trees, still wrapped. 'Yes, there's a movie here,' says Poppy. 'We ought to know which crowd to join – it ought be our destiny. Shall we ask those camera guys? Though movies – they're not news. All those guys record is shards, the pieces as they bounce, once the big pot's been dropped. Your movie—' and she turns on me. 'That had no power. Raoul's are all about that, power – even the ghosts – they knock the tables and the chairs, though they can't eat nor sit. Power's why Aspen tolerates it all – the standing like she's being portraited. The movie is for ever ...' on she talks, until I say,

'So that's the moral law? The script and the Director?' And she says,

'Well, fuck the script. That's to keep Max content. You needn't look at it.'

We wait, the people run all round, then go. I say to Poppy, 'You've stopped being Hunter – she was movement, answers immediate,' and she says,

'Hunter ended bad. She wasn't happy. What is tragic – is settled people losing work. And women. She flew on – and down she went. Not tragic, that.'

'It's a question of psychology,' I say, not believing.

'Do I need psychology too?' asks Poppy. 'I just want to dominate the scenes.'

'You'll need a man, or several,' I say.

'Don't say there's still some interest in sex!' says Poppy. 'Absolutely not. No men. And—' turning to Yves, who's slinking off, 'why shouldn't these guys here have their trees? There's nothing wrong in that.'

I say, 'Those tubes hold everything, the bad stuff too.'

We try to go back home. It wasn't like it was at first: now, more sand, more fear.

'That Armand guy – he follows you. We'll maybe get a ride back in a truck,' says Poppy, and she points. It's true, there's cops all round, their space hats shining in the sun. Like frog spawn.

'If I can't get right to the top, then I'll take flight, like Hunter. Leave the fear behind,' she says.

I say, 'I think just now, they're after Yves. To punish or exalt, it's hard to tell,' and Poppy says no doubt it's both, the cops too, split, just like the crowds of running folk – some pushed by fire, some led by hope.

'We absolutely shouldn't go in a cop truck,' I shout. Yves pushes us, we're in, the cops kiss him one-two-three, and hug.

'Yves plays for both sides,' I tell her. 'And Poppy! – no mention of the moral law!' She can't resist, she tells it all, the cops are fascinated. There's Armand, or his twin – the big ideas are frothing round: 'Yes, yes,' he says. 'The moral law can always do with cops, or else it isn't law,' and Poppy says that Yves is deep in treachery, the worm! – they say that if you're good and bad, the bad part dominates, it's harder to forgive the wrong than praise the good. And as for sacrifice – maybe we are it, the two of us.

'Well, then,' I say. 'We need to leave this truck,' but she says no, our future's flight and fear, the buildings crumble as we pass, the asphalt cracks, we see deep down to pipes and roots ... that's why Hunter flew so high, she saw the matter come apart, and if you stand upon the earth it starts to shake, the clods divide, you think it's revelation – no, it is your fall, and down and down you go, past miners' bones and Indians', and wrecks of pirate ships, and golden fetters too, like Aspen wore.

'No, no,' I say. 'Not in a police truck! Complicity is one thing, betrayal is quite worse. You watch your friends go meet their death – that is inevitable. But betraying them's another.'

'Relax, relax,' says Yves. 'You take the path that opens up – it always forks, and one branch leads you to the ever-smouldering dump. I bet these good friends here, these cops – they'll each have movies that they love, they pin their souls to them. They dream of actresses, dénouements, strippings-off – the connings and the scams.'

I say, 'Armand is maps, is countries – those promise protection, then they lock you up. They're the world, they're mouthwash. Made to be spit out ...' and on I go, as the truck ...

'Oh no!' shouts Yves – 'Mind the trees – some detonate!' And it's too late, we hit, there's bangs and lurches, we spill out – Poppy holds a gun, plastic-looking, like it's fallen off a warplane, borrowed from a museum somewhere – she's shooting, other guys are shooting back – we duck, and here's a ditch, a sewer, and we crawl on through – and here's some revolutionaries, an apartment, well-furnished too, with plants in pots, guys watching TV, some topical movie, don't catch the title, have they time to sing a song? – there's guitars all round – and here's the good-looker, making out with Poppy – there's a shot, and there is Yves, expiring on the window sill – he'd time to shoot the randy guy and so – the revolution's in our charge, the leader's passed the parcel, and Poppy's taken out the enemy ... Poor Yves, no time for last words ...

Poppy says, 'I feel I've been here already, but it's all stereotypes, has to be, or else you wouldn't orientate,' but at least we're out of Armand's custody, some scores are settled here, so mine can wait their time.

'Well,' says Yves. 'That was close. Now my friends – the guards – will help us cross the border.'

'Of course,' says Poppy. 'Those cadavers – they're not real, they're extras. The big idea goes on and on – what you must keep in mind is good and evil. That's what it's all about – and you must make the sacrifices over and over, and when you think you've reached the place you want to go – it starts again.'

I say, 'Poppy, you know Director's work so well – can't you make your movie and be satisfied?'

She pauses, then she says to me: 'No one will see yours. That you know. And if it was the same for me? No, I watch the helicopters, not the actors ...' and there they are, the helicopters buzz around the sky, and some are making movies too, and some are not.

'When they've done,' says Yves. 'The cops get a special show – *Mädchen in Uniform*, I think. It helps relax. I'll watch it with them one more time. The cast of course is fully clothed.'

*

'I told you,' Poppy says to me, alone at last. 'Guard up! Remember – big, small ideas – they never die. Directors help to keep them fresh. You think one's dead – and no! there, up it pops again, and someone puts it on the screen, or now it enters silently, sits beside your bed ...'

We're home at last. It doesn't look like home – outside it is for sure, but here, there's plants in pots, and Poppy settled in a chair.

'Here's a thing!' says Poppy, reading on a screen. 'It's Raoul's new film. It sounds like Fay and Dan – the shootouts, stuff about Tibet – here's some folks, they kiss and hug, and there's the stupas, and those hats ... The China bit is fresh.' I say,

'I don't remember that at all. There's Aspen! My! that dress – it's gold lamé, and there's a guy, a renegade, she's kissing him, seems like a major in some special corps ... It's not like Dan, but wow! those extras – from the PLA, I bet, all waving flags, I guess it's prayer-time ... and in the distance there's a train. There wasn't that in Amazonia ... That could be Gus, and Apple, happy peasants with no dialog,' and on I go, till Poppy says,

'The big idea is always fresh, that's why you need to dress it smart – besides, Dan's Indians were far too few, and dirty, probably – you need a crowd. Remember Frederson – the people go on strike, they save the banker's girl – you need them, lots of them, to move and wave their arms ...' and she goes on, until I say,

'Poppy, you're quite intelligent. Why all this stuff banal? The stereotypes, stock shots, the slaves, the liberations ...' and she says,

'It is like that. All of it. And so – forget the script, forget the news – it's style. That is what counts, the fresh, the only thing that makes a difference.'

In the room below, there's a new crowd of demented guys. Each with a single memory, held close, the only baggage they're allowed to bring. I remember 'After the ball ...' and the guy who clung to that.

Fay had said, 'They're lucky. They may have only the one, the single memory – but I forgot the thing that mattered – where I left the suitcase! That would have solved the problem ...' But she never told us what the problem was. Maybe Silverside, that cash, letting it all slip, like him, the muddy side turned down ...

I hear Poppy, as she shouts, 'I don't want to go down with the demented. I'm afraid. It's a contagion,' though I know it's not. 'I may go to make another, better movie,' she shouts down. 'But you – nothing! You're innocent. There is no case. Maybe there wasn't ever one. Forget it – it all cancels out. No case to answer, not for anyone. You've done nothing, ever, anything you've done, it runs away like water.'

I'm in the little white-washed street, below our room. The goats are tiny here, no bigger than a smallish dog.

'Or I might try something else, and steal the scene from someone you've not met,' she shouts.

'Do as you wish, my dear, my lovely Poppy,' I shout back. And there she is, I see her high up on the sill.

She spreads her arms. She seems to fly, she flies – or does she land quite soon, but out of sight, or fly, fly away like Hunter, digging her fingers in material things and out their secrets come, the structures, the components, written with atomic numbers, diagrams in blue ...?

*

As she goes, I hear my Poppy cry, 'I'll call, I'll call you on your telephone.'

About the author

John Fraser has lived in Rome since 1980. Previously, he worked in England and Canada.

www.ingramcontent.com/pod-product-compliance
Lightning Source LLC
Chambersburg PA
CBHW020550310726
48979CB00008B/1153/J
* 9 7 8 0 9 5 7 2 0 6 1 3 7 *